Helen,
Thanks so mu
Hope y



# LOUISIANA CAJUN GIRL

Donna Hankins

DONNA HANKINS
305-0852

2018
Helen H
Moore

BALBOA. PRESS
A DIVISION OF HAY HOUSE

Balboa Press books may be ordered through booksellers or by contacting:

Balboa Press
A Division of Hay House
1663 Liberty Drive
Bloomington, IN 47403
www.balboapress.com
1 (877) 407-4847



Print information available on the last page.

ISBN: 978-1-5043-5172-0 (sc)
ISBN: 978-1-5043-5174-4 (hc)
ISBN: 978-1-5043-5173-7 (e)

Library of Congress Control Number: 2016902575

Balboa Press rev. date: 03/21/2016

# Dedication

He determines the numbers of the stars and calls them each by name.

—Psalm 147:4

I consider every person and animal that has touched my life in some way a Star. These Stars came into my life shining brightly. They touched my heart and left me with special memories. When these Stars left, they brought my heart with them to the other side. I dedicate this book to you, especially my sister, Renee.

# ACKNOWLEDGMENT

Unless I had known my true calling in this world, this book might not have been written when it was. So first, I owe all the "heavenly help" and Kim O'Neill (Psychic Channel author and speaker) heartfelt thanks for opening my eyes to the knowledge of this calling.

I would like to thank my dear friend and her teenage daughter for volunteering their time and energy for their editing services. Also, my thanks to a good friend who was forever a point of contact in bringing chapter after chapter back and forth from one point to another. He happily made time for me and my new writing venture.

Thanks to several friends who read this manuscript and gave me tidbits of advice, and for the friends and family who have stood behind me, supported my writing venture, and been just as excited as I am at the completion of my first but not last book.

# CHAPTER 1

The afternoon was sunny as I sat under my favorite willow tree next to Old River in the Spring Bayou Wildlife Management Area, a hop, skip, and a jump from the boat dock and only a half mile from my house. A slight breeze kept my tousled dirty-blonde hair continuously flying in my face, and as I ran my hand through it, my mind was racing about the upcoming event.

Being born in the South had its advantages. What advantages, I didn't know, but I was sure that one day I'd figure it out. In Louisiana, humidity could be so bad that the hair closest to your neck stuck and drops of water beaded up on your forehead like you had hives. Mosquitoes were swollen with the blood of unsuspecting victims, flying close to your ear and feeding in places on your body that you didn't even know existed until you felt the burn of their bite. There were creepy-crawly things, unusual sounds, and let's not forget the larger animals in the surrounding area that you better be prepared to shoot if you had to. Yep, this part of Louisiana wasn't for the weak of heart. You had to be brought up here to know its ways. If not, you didn't have a chance in hell of making it.

I grew up on the outskirts of the small town of Marksville. Lots of people called this Cajun country, where snakes and alligators were an everyday sight to most people. This was a hunting and fishing community, and most meals came straight from the woods and the bayous to the plate. A little hot sauce on everything, a cold beer, and you were in hog heaven. A side order of hot boudin and cracklin's so good you wanted to slap your mama could bring a smile to even the grumpiest of eaters.

The women of the area were notoriously tough. You crossed a Cajun woman, and you had major trouble. They'd run you over with a tractor when you weren't looking.

Tough came in all sizes, and I was about five foot four. I was no beauty, but I did win a baby contest for having the cutest curls for a four-year-old. I was thankful my dirty-blonde curls had loosened into long waves and the constant sun had given me bright highlights cascading down my back. Daddy always said my big brown eyes were my biggest asset. Like I said, I was no raving beauty—but hell, who needed to be a beauty in the swamps of Louisiana when you could hunt right alongside any guy in the community? For me, wearing a dress and heels was like lying on a bed of nails.

Mom liked to say I needed to grow up and act like a lady. Shee, I wasn't no lady, and I didn't plan on ever being one. I was young, energetic, and happy. Just because I was twenty-three years old didn't mean I needed to change. I had my whole life ahead of me. I was free to come and go as I pleased. The world was mine for the taking. "Enjoy life" was my motto, and that meant kicking back with the guys, drinking a beer or two.

Why did I need to change? Seemed to me everyone else needed to get a life and leave me the hell alone. I was grown up enough to know what I wanted, and it didn't come in a white house with a picket fence and a bunch of kids running around. Just thinking like this made me nauseated.

"Marcie, what the heck you doing out here?" asked a familiar voice.

I turned and smiled. "I'm just taking in the scenery, Bill. Have a seat." I patted the ground next to me.

"You ready for tonight?" asked Bill.

"Well, I guess I'm as ready as I'll ever be. Who all is coming?"

"Just the gang; Frank and T Boy will meet us about eight o'clock."

"That sounds great." It was a good feeling to be accepted as one of the boys. They didn't think twice about including me in the hunt. "I think it's gonna be a good night for frogging. Moon's full, and I got my new rubber boots to try out."

"You didn't go buy those pink ones at the Dollar Store?" Bill asked with a twinkle in his eyes.

"Hell no; you know I don't go in for no pink shit. If I ain't wearing black, I ain't wearing nuttin'."

"Damn, Marcie, don't talk like that," Bill said with his head tilted and his eyebrow raised. "You know you're the cutest girl in town."

"And you need to get some glasses. You know damn well I ain't no girl.

As we laughed, Bill said, "I know; I'm just yanking your chain."

Bill was the only boy I ever let kiss me. It happened when we were about ten years old, out behind the barn. We agreed then and there we would never do that again, and we shook on it. Yuck.

"We're still friends, right?"

"Of course we are, Bill. We'll always be friends."

Bill stood about five foot eleven with sky-blue eyes and brown hair. He definitely turned some heads in town. Bill had been by my side since I could walk. Our house was welcome to most of the guys who grew up around here. Where most dads worked outside the house, my dad always seemed to have time to teach us the ways of the swamp. Yep, my dad taught us all the best things in life: hunting and fishing.

"All right, then; I'll meet y'all by the dock at eight o'clock sharp, and Bill, don't forget your knife this time."

"Well, girly, don't you forget those pretty pink boots." Bill laughed. He got up, knocked the dirt off the back of his pants, and walked back toward his truck.

I sat a while longer and then started back to the house on the old dirt road. I wondered who the hell had been mud riding out here, leaving so many ruts you could lose a family of hogs in them. I made my way back, straddling all the ruts.

"Mom, I'm back," I shouted when I walked in the door.

"Marcie, sweetie, where you been? You shouldn't be out in that heat. Your face is so red."

"Aw, Ma, I'm okay. Besides, there's a nice breeze blowing today."

"Well, get yourself cleaned up; supper will be on the table before you know it."

As I washed my hands in the kitchen sink, I could smell an array of savory dishes. It smelled like stewed chicken with lots of onions and a big pot of rice. *Mmm, is that apple pie? Shit, my mom can sure cook.*

"Please set the table, sweetie, while I take the pie out to cool."

"Okay." I paused. "Hey, Mom? Me and the boys are going frogging tonight at Spring Bayou."

"Marcie, I swear someone must have switched you at birth. I could have sworn I had a girl. I blame your dad for this, God rest his soul."

Mom continued to mumble under her breath about Daddy. Daddy taught me everything I know. He would say, "Marcie girl, you need to stand on your own two feet, 'cause ain't no one gonna take care of you but yourself. I'm gonna teach you to take care of yourself. You ain't no welfare case. We may not have much money, but you can live off the land and be happy. Be careful who you trust, and never give your heart to no man. They will just squish it under their foot and feed it to the pigs."

I had to wipe the tear coming from my eye before my mom saw. She already cried enough for the both of us. Daddy would never approve of me wimping out like this.

My God, I never knew a hurt like this. It was like my heart had been stabbed through and through with one of T Boy's hunting knives. There was such a feeling of loss in my life since my dad died.

It was a freak accident. We were hammering down some loose shingles on the roof when he lost his balance and fell headfirst into the front flower bed. We were preparing for the winter rains. It happened so fast. We were just cutting up with each other, like we always did. He had me laughing so hard, I snorted. This made us both laugh harder. When he lost his footing, I reached out to grab him, but it was too late. The look on his face was something I'll never forget. I'd never seen fear in my dad's face until that day. It was six months later now, and I swore I could still smell his cologne sometimes.

I loved sitting on the front porch in his favorite rocking chair, passing my hands across the old, worn-out paint of the chair's arms, knowing he sat there every evening for many years after supper, watching the sun go down behind the trees. Oh, my God, I missed him.

"Marcie? Marcie?" Mom repeated.

"Huh? Did you say something, Ma?"

"Where were you?" she asked.

"Not to worry. I'm just thinking if I have everything for the hunt tonight."

"Please be careful tonight, Marcie girl."

I'd been called Marcie girl so long that when I started school, I thought my first name was Marcie and my last name was Girl. Mom worries way too much. She knows I've been frogging since I was in diapers. Every boy within a mile has been here, helping Dad with the crops and hunting and fishing with us.

Shee, this is a place where everyone knows everyone. You can't sneeze at your house and expect your next door neighbor a half mile down the road not to already know all about it.

Supper was over, dishes were washed, and I was headed out the door with my new boots. I had to smile as I remembered Bill's words earlier. Pink boots? What the hell was he thinking?

Bill and I had been close friends since childhood. Actually, he'd grown up into one of the most eligible bachelors in town. He had started a small business out of his home. He loved cars, so fixing and painting cars was less a job to him than a way of life. He was very good at it too. As far as men went, I guessed he was okay.

I started my walk to the dock. It looked like someone had come by already and graded the dirt road. It looked as smooth as a baby's bottom.

As I approached the dock, I could see movement by the boat. "Hey, everyone, we ready to push off?"

"We're just waiting on T Boy," Bill said.

We all knew that T Boy had the furthest to come to go frogging. He and his parents lived way past where the road ended. We all considered him and his family pure swamp people. We always teased him, saying he lived so far out in the woods that you had to pipe in sunshine. T Boy didn't have much schooling and probably had the thickest accent of us all. He was also the quietest of the bunch. Since his family didn't have money and he didn't finish school, we just figured he was embarrassed about his circumstances.

One day T Boy just said, "Mais, I's jus ain't got nuttin' to say. What be wrong wit' dat?" We all laughed.

Here he came now. T Boy was anything but little. He must have stood six foot tall without shoes. In fact, I couldn't remember if I ever saw him in shoes. His clothes were ill-fitting hand-me-downs with holes. In fact, if I had to say who I thought he looked like, I'd say he looked like a big overgrown Huckleberry Finn. He had dirty-blond hair with big soft curls, freckles, and the nicest hazel eyes you ever wanted to see. T Boy was the wisest of us all when it came to hunting and fishing in the swamps. It was like he could sense the animals' every move. I often wondered if he couldn't read their minds. When it came down to it, his family only lived off the land, so I guess he learned it all from his dad and his dad's dad, way back into history.

"Come on, T Boy, we're pushing off," said Frank.

T Boy ran and tripped when he jumped off the dock into the boat, almost throwing us all in the bayou. Of all of us I'd have to say that Frank was the smartest of us all. He had already gotten several years of college under his belt. He wanted to be a pharmacist. We only saw Frank on the weekends. He was very level headed and didn't have much of a sense of humor. Frank had dark hair and dark eyes and stood about five foot nothing.

"Well, let's get that motor running and stop all this messing around," I said with a smile.

"Keep your shirt on, Marcie, you know old Betsy is cold natured."

Bill would sweet-talk his old boat motor, rubbing her and telling her if she would start, he would give her a good cleaning inside and out in the morning. I looked to see the smiles on Frank and T Boy's faces as we watched Bill do his magic with this cantankerous old motor. After several more yanks and a couple more nice words, she started right up.

"There she goes, just a-purring like a kitten," Bill said with a crocked grin.

We started our journey down the river. It was pitch black with about a million mosquitoes and a repetitious array of nighttime noises. If you stopped to listen, it would be deafening.

Maybe fifteen or twenty minutes down the river Bill stopped the motor and turned to put on the trolling motor. Each one of us took our positions and got ready for our first frog as we drifted slowly toward the bank. We'd done this so many times, we were like a well-oiled machine; we all knew our jobs. Now was the time to be quiet and keep our eyes peeled. It was my job to shine the light on the riverbank. T Boy was positioned on the side the boat, and Frank had his net in case T Boy missed his mark. Needless to say Frank never had to do anything, because T Boy was the best I ever saw at frogging, hunting, fishing or anything from the Cajun way of life.

Bill slowly maneuvered the flat-bottom boat around an old cypress stump, almost running us onto the bank. "There's one," I whispered. I pointed to a clump of brush by the water's edge.

I kept my light steady on the huge bullfrog just a couple of feet away. T Boy snatched up the frog just behind his head.

"Cho co, mais dis is sum good eating, yeah. I's can taste the gravy now."

We all knew what T Boy was saying. To T Boy, if you had meat you had to have gravy. Personally I like my legs fried, but gravy sounds good too.

It could be a tricky thing to come up on a bullfrog like that. You had to keep the spotlight on him the whole time, blinding him while someone held a net out front in case he jumped and another came in from the back to grab.

"Another couple dozen more and we can go," Frank said.

The night was good, just a little muggy. There was the slightest breeze, which made the river jump up against the boat in an easy rocking motion.

"There's nothing like living off the land," I said.

"You sound like your old man," said Bill.

"Yeah, times like this I really miss him."

It got quiet on the boat with that comment. I think we were all thinking the same thing. There was always an empty seat on the boat since Dad died. He was just one of the boys, along with the rest of us.

Almost two hours passed when we had caught our quota and were headed back. "The frogs were plentiful tonight," I said as I looked at the moving sack on the floor of the boat.

In the distance we could see a light in the woods. "Who you suppose that is?" asked Bill.

"I think it's on land," Frank murmured.

We were so far back on Spring Bayou it would be real unusual to find a light out here unless it was another boat.

"Maybe someone is camping out," Frank said as he squinted to see in the dark.

"It could be," I said.

"Mais, it could be dat crazy man back dar," T Boy said with his thick Cajun accent.

We had all heard stories of a crazy man who lived deeper in the woods than T Boy. They said he practiced black magic, voodoo or something, and to see him up close would scare you to the grave. Other than that, that's all we ever heard about this stranger. Never knew anyone who had even seen him. But with the description I'd heard about this man, I didn't think I ever wanted to run into him.

It lingered in our minds what that light could have been as we slowly made our way back to the dock. We docked the boat with a promise of a frog leg supper tomorrow night at Bill's camp on the river.

# CHAPTER 2

Next day, the morning sun was streaking through my bedroom window before I got out of bed. Lying there with my eyes open, trying to focus, I thought I saw something in the corner of my room. I jumped up to a sitting position, straining my eyes and searching the corner for any movement. Nothing. *I must be losing my mind. What's that smell?* I sat at the edge of the bed sniffing the air. *It smells like— Mmm. It smells good and kind of familiar. Oh, I know this scent; it's Old Spice.* That was exactly what my dad wore.

"Oh, Daddy, I said out loud, "I miss you more than life itself."

It seemed that as soon as I spoke, the smell was gone. It was as though I'd imagined the whole thing. *Did I just smell Old Spice? What was in the corner of the room? Did something really move? I swear, I've totally lost it. Maybe I'm still dreaming. Oh well, I can't just sit here all day wondering about my sanity.* "I'm out of here. I have work to do. The chores won't get done by themselves. Why in the world am I talking to myself? Man, that must have unnerved me more than I thought."

I dressed up for the day, blue jeans and an old navy blue T-shirt, and ran into the kitchen. There was Mom cooking fried cleeps, which Cajuns call fried bread dough. Fresh cleeps was one of those Cajun family secrets handed down from each generation's girls to the next.

She had been up early, heating her small cast iron skillet with hot grease. As she heated the grease, she would slowly pull on the fresh, raw bread dough that she had made by hand the day before until she had a perfect saucer size shape. She would poke a couple of holes in the dough and place it in the hot grease. She would turn the dough until it was golden brown. Then she'd wrap them in a paper towel, ready to grab and go. They would be hot, crisp on the outside, and moist on the inside. Sometimes when there was time I would sprinkle powdered sugar on them or dip them in some fresh cane syrup. I remembered my dad dipping his cleep in his coffee. Hey, whatever floats your boat.

I was finishing my cleep by the time I got to the barn. There are chickens to feed and eggs to pick. Then it was out to the pastures to throw some hay. The other half of my dad's land was farmed. Mom and I had been lucky to find someone to plant our acreage on a percentage bases. Dad left a large sum of money to live off of, so really there were no worries. Who would have dreamed that Dad would think of us like that? We never knew he had taken out an insurance policy years ago.

The rest of the day was uneventful. With all the chores out of the way, I climbed on my four-wheeler and rode around the property, checking on everything and making sure everything was in order. Satisfied that I had completed my daily chores to the best of my ability, like my dad had taught me, I headed back to the kitchen to wash my hands in the kitchen sick. I tied my hair back and started chopping some onions for tonight. The sun was setting behind the trees. I was watching out the window and saw shadows lurking behind every tree as I chopped the onions. I kept my eyes half on the onions and half out the window. Ever since Dad had died, I tried not to miss a sunset.

I packed some other cooking essentials. Then I yelled, "See you later, Mom."

"Okay, be careful out there, and don't be too late," she called back.

I walked slowly, enjoying yet another night with a cool breeze. I had the strangest feeling that someone was following me. I kept walking straight ahead, trying not to act scared. After all, I was Marcie, my father's daughter. *Fear* is a four-letter word that is not allowed in our vocabulary. How many times had I heard my dad say that?

*Maybe the guys are playing a trick on me or something. Maybe it's an escaped convict from the parish jail. Gee, Marcie, you are totally losing it; get a grip. There is no one out there. Just because its dark doesn't mean there is something out there. Why in the hell am I talking to myself?*

I found myself frozen in my tracks. The feeling of a presence was so strong, it was like someone was about to jump out and grab me. I slowly looked behind me to see who was following and saw nothing. *Maybe if I yell out, they will know that I know they are there.*

"Hello? I asked. "Is anyone there?"

"Marcie girl," someone whispered. I jumped. It sounded like someone right next to me, but I could see no one. My eyes strained to see from my left to my right. There was so much movement in the trees that I felt like my mind was playing tricks on me.

"What? Who's out there?" I demanded out loud. No answer. "Hello?" I asked again.

"Marcie girl, I'm here. Can you see me?"

"Who's there?" I demanded again.

The voice continued, "I'm sorry, Marcie girl"

*My God, that sounded just like my dad.* "Daddy? Is that you?" I pleaded.

"I'm sorry for leaving you so soon."

"Daddy, where are you? I can't see you." My mind raced. How could this be? My insides started to shake. "Daddy, please, where are you?"

Warm tears started running down my face. My heart was beating so hard and loud, I thought that the "voice of my dad" could hear it.

"Marcie girl, please don't cry. I'm always with you."

Again, I thought, *How can this be? No!* I put my hands over my ears and ran down the old dirt road straight to the dock.

"No, no, no. This can't be."

I looked behind me when I reached the dock and saw no one following me. I sat on the dock looking over my shoulder, searching the darkness for any kind of movement while I hung my feet off the edge of the dock. My whole body shook as I waited for the gang to get there, trying to make since of it all. I was continually looking behind me for anything out of the ordinary. My heart was still racing. I tried to calm my nerves. I looked down and saw my hands shaking. Was someone playing a joke on me? It sounded like my dad. *But he died six months ago. Surely I didn't hear what I thought I heard.* My shaking was so bad that my teeth were chattering.

I heard something behind me. *Someone's coming. Oh my God, who or what could it be?* I scrambled from my seated position and braced myself. I didn't know what to expect next. My breath caught in my throat. I just knew I was ready for the next encounter, whatever it might be. *It sure can't be good. After all, who hears dead people on lonely dark roads in the middle of the night?* I wiped my face and braced myself for a fight. *Whether dead or not, they don't know who they're messing with. I'll fight to the end.*

My chest was bowed out like a banty rooster with my hands clenched into tight fists, waiting for a fight.

"Hey, Marcie," Bill called. "Looks like you're ready to fight some alligators."

I let out my held breath. My body started to go limp, and I almost lost my balance. I couldn't believe how scared I was. I had never been so glad to see someone in all my life. If Bill only knew just how ready I was to kick some Cajun ass. I had to laugh at myself. *Surely this was just the dark playing tricks on me. I won't say a word about what just happened, or they'll send me away in a straitjacket.*

Bill and Frank were walking toward me, and out the corner of my eye I could see T Boy was coming in from another direction down the road to meet us.

*The gang's all here; what a relief.*

"Marcie, you look kinda pale. You okay?" Bill asked.

Everyone stopped what they were doing to glance at me.

"I'm just fine, boys. I'm ready for some frog legs." I winked at Bill and the boys.

I had a great poker face. That was something my dad taught me growing up. Never let the enemy see your weakness. In this case, never let the guys see you're a girl. I looked in the large pot T Boy was carrying. He had already cleaned the frogs and had them soaking in some homemade secret sauce. I could smell the hot sauce from the pot. T Boy would never tell us what his secret sauce was, but it didn't matter; we knew it was good.

We all guessed at least one of T Boy's secret ingredients: hot sauce. *Man, these little babies are going to be hot.*

I smiled. *Ah, now this is real,* I thought.

We jumped in the flat-bottom boat, taking our normal seats, and headed down the river to Bill's camp. It was just up a ways behind some old cypress stumps to the left. The moon was still out, nice and bright. It made the walk to Bill's camp a little easier, even with flashlights. We climbed out of the boat and followed a narrow dirt path a short piece through the woods to the camp. Bill's camp hadn't seen paint in years. It stood a good twenty feet off the ground in case of high waters.

We climbed up the stairs to the porch. I looked back to see if anyone was following us. I was so spooked that I just felt like I wasn't alone. Not like being with the guys. It was a different feeling, like just a strong sense of something hiding in the dark, watching.

"What's the matter, Marcie? Did you forget something in the boat?" asked Frank.

"No, Frank, just looking at the full moon that's all. —So who brought the beers?"

"Don't look at me. You know I got church tomorrow, and I'd get my butt chewed good if I drank tonight."

We all looked at Frank. We knew his family well. Frank's family was his driving force. His family was well respected and very strict on him. They had his life all planned out: college first, then marriage and grandkids—you know, the American Dream. Frank toed the line. He knew that without his family's support, there wouldn't be a paid college education.

T Boy spoke up. "Well, dat jus' leave mo' beer fo' me." We all laughed.

We all headed for Bill's backpack to grab a beer and get to cooking. Dinner was fried and stewed frog legs, French fries, my secret dipping sauce, and a pot of rice. We lit every lantern in the place to see. There was no electricity out this far in the woods.

Soon we each grabbed a seat at the old worn-out table and began to eat.

After a while of small talk, I just had to ask, "Do y'all believe in life after death?"

Frank was first to respond. He said, "Yes, the Bible speaks of that."

"That's not what I mean, Frank. Do you believe people who die can come back?"

"No, of course not," Frank said.

Bill cocked his head my way. "What's up with that question, Marcie? I never would have thought you of all people would ask a question like that."

"Oh, Bill, I'm just yanking your chain," I said with a laugh. "I was just having fun and trying to break the silence."

"You know, when the food is good, you ain't going to hear one word from us," Frank said. "We're too busy stuffing our face."

Everyone seemed amused with that remark at least for a minute. But inside I really wanted to know. How could I bring something up like that in front of the guys? *But who can I talk to about this?*

T Boy didn't even seem to even hear what I'd asked and kept on eating. After several more hours of small talk, dishes, and a couple more beers, we decided to head back. We finished out our night, packed up our extras, and set out for the boat. There was still that feeling of someone watching, but I wasn't about to mention it. I just wanted to shake it off and get back home.

We said our good-nights at the dock, and Bill walked me part of the way home. Seemed there was something on his mind, he was so quiet. I was just glad I had company.

"Okay, Marcie, I'll see you later."

"Good night, Bill, see you later."

Once Bill left my side, I found myself alone, hesitating and dreading the walk on the dark, spooky road. It was considerably unnerving. I found myself trying to tiptoe past the spot of the ghostly encounter earlier. As if anyone could actually hear me out here with all the wildlife. Kind of like maybe I would wake up the dead. I smiled at myself.

I was so glad to get home and in my warm cozy bed. That night I tossed and turned. I kept reliving the encounter over and over in my head. But I finally drifted into a deep sleep.

In my dream I could see a wonderful place. The lake was clear, and the sky was bluer than I'd ever seen. I sat on a fallen log by the edge listening to the birds and feeling the warm sun on my back. Everything seemed so vibrant and crisp, and the colors stood out vividly. *This has to be the most beautiful place I've ever seen in my whole life.*

Suddenly I caught movement out of the corner of my eye. I looked to see someone walking my way. *Who is that? There is something familiar about that walk. Oh, my God, it looks like my dad walking up to me.* He started getting closer and coming into view even more. There he was. He stood before me just as real as the last time I saw him.

"Daddy?" I asked as I stood to my feet.

"It's okay, Marcie girl. I'm not here to hurt you."

I stuttered as I said, "Daddy, I-I never thought you would hurt me." I slowly lifted my hand to his face. I just had to touch him. He felt real. He was warm, and the scent of Old Spice was upon him. Tears filled my eyes as I grabbed him with all my strength. This was no dream.

"Is it really you, Daddy?" I whispered.

*Of course it is*, I thought. I buried my face in his shoulder and squeezed him even harder. How could I ever let him go? *What if he leaves again?* My mind was torn two ways. One side was accepting this unusual dream, and the other part of me doubted everything.

How could this be? But it just didn't matter. He was here now, with me, in this beautiful place.

It was as though he knew what I was thinking. He grabbed my shoulder and pushed me from him with his face just inches from me. "My little Marcie girl, sit with me while I try to explain."

"Daddy, I've missed you so much."

"I know, my little Marcie girl," Dad said with sadness in his face. "I feel what you feel. I also feel your mom. She mourns me tremendously."

"I know, I hear her at night crying. But I don't let on that I know."

As we sat on the log together, looking in each other's eyes, Dad continued to speak. I know my eyes were as big as saucers as I listened.

"Marcie girl, I've come to you in your dreams because I feel this is the best way to communicate with you without scaring you."

"Daddy, was that you on the road tonight?"

"Yes, my little girl, it was me. But I didn't mean to scare you. I've been with you since day one."

"How, Daddy? How?"

"I can only tell you what you are ready to hear. No man can know or comprehend God and His ways fully. Man cannot even comprehend His infiniteness, His glory. His ways are so much higher than ours that it would be impossible for anyone to completely understand the how, the what, the where, or the when that I am even with you right now. What I can tell you is that He loves you as I do. He has never left our side for a moment. He sends His angels to minister to us, to help us on our journey. Marcie girl, there is no death. There is only a laying down of your flesh. We are not this earthen vessel we put on. We are so much more."

I was confused. "Daddy, this doesn't sound like you. You would never have talked about things like this."

"I know, Marcie girl. I was blinded by the flesh. I didn't realize who I was. It wasn't until I left the body that I realized just how wrong I was as a human on the earth. I didn't even finish my life work. I'm so sorry, Marcie girl for the things I taught you. I was wrong. I had this big chip on my shoulder that made it even harder to see the truth. I couldn't see past my own insecurities to see or feel or teach you the truth."

"Daddy, what are you talking about? What truth?"

He laughed. "Marcie girl, I can't explain the universe in one dream. But there is someone who can help you see things a little better."

"Who?"

"You will find him where you least expect. Follow the light."

"Light? What light, Daddy?"

Slowly my dear precious dad was fading away right before my eyes.

"No, please don't leave me again. Please don't leave," I begged.

Again he said, "Follow the light."

"Daddy, don't go!" I yelled. "Daddy! Daddy!"

"Sweetie, it's okay. You're having a bad dream."

I woke to find my mom sitting next to me on the crumpled bed. She was wiping the tears and sweat from my face. "It's okay, it's just a dream," she said with great concern.

"No, Mom, it was real. It was Daddy. He's okay. He's alive and well in, in—I don't know where he was, but he was okay. He was alive and happy. He looked great, Mom."

"Marcie, please don't talk like that." Mom's face had lost all its color, and she had a strange look on her face.

"Mom, he feels your pain. He knows how you feel, how you cry for him."

"Stop it, Marcie, stop it!" she yelled as she jumped up from my bed. "You're talking nonsense. I won't sit here and listen to this. You had a dream, and that's all there is to it." She stomped out of the room and closed the door behind her.

I sat up in bed to look at the time. It was 3:33 a.m. I wasn't nearly sleepy after that dream. I put on my robe and slippers and headed to the kitchen for some warm milk. I sat for an hour drinking my warm milk and going over the dream.

What did he mean, "Follow the light"? What light? I'd find my answers where? From somewhere I would least expect. What was he talking about? Or was it even real? Maybe this was just a dream. Maybe Mom was right.

I headed back to bed feeling better. *Yes, it was just a dream. It was all a dream. It sure seemed real though. In fact, it seems more real than what I feel right now. No, it was a dream, just a dream. Here we go again. I'm talking to myself again.* I lay back down in my queen-size bed, and after a short while I was sound asleep.

# CHAPTER 3

Days had passed since that dream. I decided to write everything down that I had witnessed and thought during the whole ordeal. Mom never mentioned anything else about that night, and I didn't either.

I had finished my chores and headed to the dock to do some fishing. As I sat in the late afternoon under the trees near the dock, I watched the rippled water sway the red bobber on the line from my old cane pole resting on my lap. The combination of the sun glistening off the water and the gentle movement seemed to put me into some kind of daze. Time slipped away from me. When I finally woke up from this hypnotized state of mind, I realized the sun was setting. I was confused for a moment. Where was I? *I can't believe I sat and watched the water all afternoon and without one bite.* I picked up my line to see no bait. Where was my bait? Did I even bait my hook? What was I doing? The sun was setting, and the shadows were coming out from the darkness. I started to gather my gear when I noticed a light across the bayou. Then what my father had said came back to me. Follow the light. Surely he didn't mean a light in the woods, but what if that was it?

I dropped my gear, ran to the dock, and jumped into the only boat tied there. It just so happened to be Bill's boat. I tried to start the motor. That damn motor, just as cantankerous as usual. If only Bill was here to sweet-talk it. I had to smile with the thought of a grown man talking to an outboard motor. On the third pull, the motor caught.

I made my way across the bayou to where I'd seen the light. I ran up on the shore with the boat and jumped out. Then I accidentally tripped against the side of the boat and fell face first on the ground.

Dazed, I got up, tied off the boat, and grabbed a flashlight, and off I went into the woods. "What if this is the crazy man of the swamp? What will I say to whoever it is when they catch me following them?" I had to stop myself when I realized I was talking to myself out loud, again.

The woods took on a life of its own at night. Animal sounds everywhere, movements behind trees and shadows in all directions. Vines tripping you and moss brushing on your face and shoulders like a light touch from an angel.

*Where is the light?* I turned out my light to see if I could see ahead of me. "There. There it is," I whispered to myself. Walking a little faster, I almost tripped and fell again. "Big dummy, put on your flashlight," I said aloud.

Soon I knew I'd walked about twenty minutes. Of course time has no meaning in the woods. It could really have been five minutes as far as I knew. *Where can this light be going? Wait, I think the movement has stopped.* As I inched in closer and closer, I could see an outdoor camp fire. Behind the fire was an old camp. Looked worse than Bill's. I stood behind a tree shaking, with sweat dripping off my brow. *Now what do I do? Do I go knock on the door of the cabin? Then what? Do I say, "Avon calling"? What do I do?*

My mind was racing. I started to feel stupid for listening to myself and following this person out in the middle of the woods. Just then I saw someone come out of the cabin and head to the fire. It wasn't anyone I recognized. He sat close to the fire and moved some logs here and there, giving the wood some more air to burn. The fire was crackling and small sparks were flying in the air like tiny tinker bells.

"Hello out there, would you like to join me?" a soft male voice said.

*Is he talking to me? How can he see me? Maybe if I don't talk he'll know he made a mistake.*

The voice by the fire said, "I know you're there. You can come sit here; I won't bite."

*Oh my God, he really knows I'm here. What do I do?* I hesitantly inched out from behind the trees. The man never looked up from the fire as I walked over.

My hair was a tangled mess with leaves and small twigs, and dirt was smudged on my face from when I hit the ground. My pants were torn at the knee also, and there was blood sticking my pants to my leg. I must have looked a sight.

I tried to straighten my shirt. I shook out my hair, trying to dislodge the mess, and pulled it back before I sat down on an old log facing the fire about four feet from the man. It was as though the whole world stopped. The woods fell silent. The only noise I could hear was the crackling fire. The quiet was deafening between me and the stranger.

I broke the silence. "How did you know I was there?"

After what seemed forever, the man finally looked up from the fire and smiled. "You followed my light, right?" he asked.

"Yes, why?"

"Well, did you think I couldn't see yours?" he said with a crooked smile.

I felt so dumb. Of course he saw me coming.

"I not only saw you; I heard you. You sounded like a herd of elephants tramping through the woods. I think your dad taught you better than that."

"What? You know my dad?" I asked with a gasp.

"I've met him a time or two," the man responded.

"So who are you?" I asked.

"My name is Jim, Jim Norman," the man said, "and you're Marcie girl, right?"

"I've never met you. No one calls me that but my family. How could you know who I am or my name?" I demanded.

"Like I said, I've met your dad a time or two."

After a while I asked, "So Jim, are you from here? 'Cause I don't recall seeing you before."

"I'm from here and there," he said. This man Jim seemed to not want to give to much information about himself. I figured he meant he traveled a lot and had lived many places.

Jim slowly stirred the fire, and then turned to look at me. "So what are you doing out here?"

"I don't know," I replied. "I saw a light, so I followed it."

"Do you often follow lights in the middle of the woods," asked Jim.

I smiled. "Actually, yours is the first light I've ever followed."

"That's good to know." We both laughed.

Jim had a very kind face. He was about five foot eight with hazel eyes and chestnut hair. His hair was long and tied back in a ponytail close to his neck. He looked to be in his mid to late forties. He was dressed nicely, considering he looked like he lived out in the woods in the worst camp I had ever seen. He was not another T Boy. This man seemed educated and different. I didn't know how, but different.

"Have you been living in the woods here a long time?" I asked.

"It's been home for me for several years, off and on," Jim said. "I travel, and this is one of my favorite spots."

"Really, you travel? So where do you go?" I asked, trying to carry on a conversation.

"I've gone to many places," Jim said.

I felt he was avoiding my questions for some reason.

"Marcie, again, why are you out here?" Jim's face seemed concerned as he asked me the question.

"I don't know, Jim. I guess I'm just curious."

"Okay, Marcie, if you say so," he said, with a note of sarcasm.

We sat in silence for a while. I found myself getting restless and uneasy, wondering what I was doing. Finally, I stood up. "I guess I should go," I said.

"Would you like me to walk you back to your boat?" Jim asked.

I looked behind me in the darkness of the woods and really hated to admit I was a little afraid to be out there, so reluctantly I said, "Yes, that would be nice."

I followed Jim back down the same path I had taken just minutes ago. There wasn't a breeze in the trees, and the humidity made the air feel thick and sticky. After what seemed like hours, we were back at the boat. Being in the dark in the woods always made walks seem long. Jim started to walk away without even a word.

"Jim?" I asked. "Would it be all right if I come visit you again?" What was I saying? Why would I want to come visit this man I'd never met before, who lived like a hermit in the woods?

"You are welcome to come again, but think about why you want to come back, Marcie. Think real hard about it." Then he turned and left.

I got back in the boat but had to sit there and wonder what had just transpired and what had been going on in my life lately. Was Jim the light my dad talked about? Why was Jim so different? On top of everything else, there was something familiar about him. Who was he? Why, six months after my dad's death, was all this going on? Was it a dream I had, or was it really my dad in the dream? *Shoot, maybe I'm in the dream now. It could have been me who fell off the roof, and all this is a result of brain damage. Maybe I'm in a coma in the hospital right now.* I started to giggle. *Man, when my mind takes off it sure makes no sense. I didn't fall off the roof. But this sure has been a strange time for me, and once more I find I'm talking out loud to myself over and over again. I've totally dropped off the earth, really.*

# CHAPTER 4

It had been several days since my encounter with Jim. The last several days had been pretty uneventful, daily chores and just living life as usual. I was thankful for normal.

I found myself sitting under my favorite willow tree a half mile from my house on Old River to just contemplate how much of a fool I had acted, traipsing in the woods following Jim and not even having mind enough to tell him why I was there. *He seems to know more than he lets on. In fact, I'm sure he knows why I was there. So when I go back, do I spill the beans about the dream or all the weird stuff and tell him he is the light I'm to follow? Or do I play it cool and act like a dumb blonde or a nosy Cajun woman of the bayous? What can I lose by telling him the truth? That's it. I'll tell him the truth.*

"Hey, lazy bumpkin, seems every time I see you, you're sitting under that old willow tree," Bill said from a distance, walking toward me. "I haven't seen you too much lately. Is everything all right?"

"Oh yeah, you know me. I've been working, and we got calves about to drop. So I've been staying close to home."

"So how many calves you expecting this spring?" Bill asked.

"Oh, I guess about a dozen, if everything goes all right. Remember last year when Dad and I had to help deliver a couple calves in the barn?"

"I remember how excited you were with all that," Bill said.

Bill really wasn't into blood, guts, or afterbirth. I gave him a small grin as I remembered that about him. He almost passed out in elementary school when he cut his foot on a broken bottle at the Indian Creek field trip. I had to lay it on thick when that happened. I would tease him unmercifully. "Oh look, Bill, it's not bleeding anymore." Then he would look and start to sway because his foot would be gushing blood. I just loved teasing him.

"So Marcie, what are we doing this weekend?" he asked.

"Well, I don't know. What do you and the boys want to do?"

Bill cleared his throat. "I, I was wondering if maybe you would like to go to dinner with me Saturday night?" His voice was shaking.

"Bill, what's wrong with you? Are you asking me on a date?" I smiled to see him so nervous.

"Well, kind of."

"What do you mean, kind of?" I teased.

"You and I have been friends a long time. We hunt, fish, and frog together. You know I'm there to help you at the farm whenever you're in need. Marcie, I haven't done all this just because we're friends."

Bill's look was so intent that it made my smile fade.

"Bill, you can't be serious. You know that I'm not like that. Daddy always said to keep my head on. Never be ruled by feelings but by my mind. Going out on a date like that just is not an option. You are only kidding me, right?"

Bill laughingly said, "Of course I'm not serious. I'm just pulling your leg, Marcie."

He turned his head away from me and said, "Okay, enough playing around. Give me a call when your cows start birthing, and I'll try to give you a hand." He got up and started to walk away.

"All right, then," I said. "I'll see you later, okay?"

"Sure" was the only response.

I watched as he slowly walked away. *Did I hurt his feelings? What a strange thing to ask me. He knows full well that I'll never date or give my heart away to any man. My dad taught me well. He said love was an illusion of self and not to give in to it—to stay strong, keep my head on my shoulders, and be self-sufficient.*

*Tomorrow is Saturday; I will make my way back to Jim's. I just have to go. It's like my very being is pulling me there. Maybe he is the light. Or maybe I've lost my mind. Maybe all this is just a dream. But I have to know.*

Mom was in the kitchen cooking when I got home. It smelled so good.

"Hi, Mom, smells like a roast cooking."

"It is," she said with a smile.

"With potatoes, carrots, onions, and a pot of rice?" I asked as I lifted the lids on all the pots.

"You know, Marcie, it wouldn't hurt you to learn how to cook."

"Mom, I know how to cook. I just prefer not to."

"You'll be twenty-four next month, and maybe we should have a talk about you settling down and getting married."

"I just walked in the door, and besides, we've talked about this before." I said, exasperated.

"Yeah, we did," said Mom, "but you're getting older, and it's time to make some changes."

"Mom, really. You know I love you, but settling down just is not in my future."

She tilted her head and gave me a look. "Marcie girl, could you explain why this is not in your future?"

"You remember what Daddy always told me, about not trusting or relying on anyone. He said you'll always get hurt."

"Marcie, I loved your dad very much, but he was wrong in telling you that. You've got to try and give your heart to someone one day. If you can't love, then what is life for? If you can never trust anyone, then you should just go find yourself a cave and live in it."

"Okay, Mom, are you finished? I really have some things to do today. Can we just eat, please?"

"All right, sweetie, but if you change your mind, you know that Bill is a good catch."

"Mom, please, end of discussion," I demanded.

The rest of the meal was pretty uneventful, and the air was thick with the conversation we'd just had. It kind of made the roast a little hard to swallow. *I know she means well, but didn't she learn anything from Dad? She heard him preach enough. If she had a problem with what he said, why didn't she say anything?*

Next day, I was happy to be out of the house and headed to Jim's. It was good to see the boat sitting at the dock and ready to go. Maybe that motor would start without sweet-talking her today. I got in, and on the first pull she purred like a kitten. In seconds I was headed across the bayou. Spring Bayou was a large body of water surrounded by woods. In fact, it was so large that it sat behind three towns, and it was big enough to hide a family of Bigfoot, and no one would ever come across them.

I docked the boat by an old cypress stump. I sat for a few minutes looking at all the trees before me. Most were hung with moss, giving everything an eerie look. I was thankful that it wasn't dark yet. The walk through the woods was easier in the daylight. I could see for a long way.

Jim's place was not an easy trip. Most camps overlooked the river. But his camp was set back and really secluded.

I didn't know why, but I trusted this man. He could be a crazy serial killer hiding in the swamps of Louisiana. *But somehow he just doesn't seem like that.*

I walked up the steps to Jim's place. *What a dump,* I thought. I knocked quietly and swallowed hard, wondering what I would say.

"Come in," Jim said.

I walked in and was very surprised to see that the inside of his place didn't look anything like the outside. The inside was clean and looked like a new home. I gasped at the contrast from outside to inside.

Jim looked up from reading and said, "You look surprised."

"I am. Jim, this place is great. Are you going to do the outside too?"

"What, and give someone the idea that I'm not a Cajun swamp man? I got to blend in around here. Of course you know what people say about me, don't you?"

"No, what?" I asked.

"That I'm a crazy man, and I practice voodoo out here."

I started to laugh. "You mean you're the crazy swamp man? They say to even look on you would scare you to your grave," I said as I continued to laugh.

He smiled back. "Oh, so that's what people are saying now about me."

I sat across from Jim in a big overstuffed chair. "How did you get all this furniture here?"

Jim winked. "It wasn't easy."

How strange, Jim's furniture was not nearly camp furniture. It looked like the kind of furniture you'd find in a real nice home in the city.

"Okay, Marcie, to what do I owe this visit?"

"Well Jim, I—I wanted to thank you for your hospitality the other night." I said in a shaky voice.

Jim put his book down, took off his glasses, and stared at me. "Marcie, why are you afraid to tell me why you're really here?"

"I don't know what you're talking about," I said. "What makes you think that?"

"You know where the door is," he said with a funny look on his face.

"What? You're kicking me out?" I said in disbelief. Furious, I jumped from the chair and stormed out. I slammed the door and stomped down the stairs.

Then something stopped me in my tracks. All I could do was to relive what Daddy had said. "Follow the light."

"Damn," I said under my breath. "Shit, shit, shit. Okay, Marcie, you can do this. Just turn around and go back in there and tell the man. What's he going to do—kick you out?" I laughed aloud because that was exactly what he'd done, and I didn't even mention the weird stuff. *Once all this is over, I really need to get myself checked out by a good psychiatrist. This talking out loud to my self is really weird.*

I went up the stairs, drew in a deep breath, and slowly walked back in. Jim was waiting for me, just as if he knew I was coming back.

I sat across from him and said with my head down, "You're going to think me crazy."

"Well, you're talking to the crazy man of the swamp. I doubt I will consider anything you say crazy."

"I think you're the light," I said.

"I'm the light; what kind of light?" Jim asked.

"I'm not sure. My dad said follow the light. So the other night I followed the light. I think you're that light."

"You mean you followed me because your dad said to follow a flashlight in the middle of the woods?" Jim asked.

"Well, he didn't say what kind of light. He just said I would find some answers if I follow the light. I saw your light, so I followed. Now you know why I'm here. I told you, you'd find me crazy."

"So you say your dad told you to follow the light?"

"Yes, he did."

"Was that recently?" Jim asked.

"Yes, in a dream I had the other night."

Under his breath he said, "He told me he'd get you here."

"Did you say he told you I was coming?" I asked.

"Yes, he did."

"How?" I asked with my jaw falling slack.

Jim tilted his head and leaned closer to me. "You remember when I said I've seen your dad a time or two."

"Yes, I remember." There was silence in the air. I spoke up. "I thought you knew my dad from a long time ago."

"No, not really," Jim said. "In fact, it was recently."

"You saw my dad recently?"

"Yes, he said he would get you here. I just didn't know how he would pull that off, but here you are."

"What are you saying, Jim?"

"I'm saying I talk to people who are not here anymore."

"You mean dead people?" I asked.

"Well no, not exactly. People never die, Marcie, they just change. I've been talking to people on the other side ever since I lost my sister to cancer twenty years ago. Not sure what started it all. It could have been the stress of my sister having cancer, or maybe something just opened up in me. I'm not sure why, but I've learned a lot over the last twenty years, since this all started. I believe your father wants you to learn how to communicate with him. I know he has things to tell you, and I think he wants me to help you understand."

"Jim, are you sure about all this? Do you know what my dad has to say?"

"I do know that he is sorry."

"Sorry, for what, Jim? He was a great dad. We were very close."

"He also does not want you to be afraid of him," Jim said.

"Well, that is easier said than done. This is all so weird to me."

"I realize that," Jim said with so much understanding that I had to really look hard at him to try to see where he was coming from.

He went on, "You have to realize I felt the same way when I first smelled my sister's perfume after her death. How I could hear her talking to me for weeks and just thought it was my memory playing tricks on me. I couldn't believe what was happening at the time. I read books galore; I traveled and went to seminars and just did anything I could to try and understand what was going on with me. I was told by some people that I was possessed; some said I needed to go to the mental institution, and a few have just accepted all this as a part of my life as a special gift.

"Marcie, this can be a part of your life too, if you want. We all have the opportunity to talk to relatives on the other side or even our angels or spirit guides. We are never alone. Did you think God or the Universe whatever you personally call Him would just leave us here on this planet with no help?"

I quietly listened to all Jim was saying. I had no idea what to make of it all. Jim was like a wise old man. All I could think was *I'm not crazy. I did hear my dad on the road, and I did see him in my dream.*

Jim continued, "There is so much out there, Marcie. Just because you can't see something, it doesn't mean it not there. It's what you call faith. Faith is believing in something, anything that your physical body cannot comprehend. If you decide to take this journey and let me teach you what I know, you will be ridiculed and thought strange, and people will even say you need to see a shrink.

"We didn't understand cell phones when they came out or that you could be seen from a satellite in outer space. Who could comprehend that? But it's true nonetheless. We as humans think we can understand the mind of God and the universe. How do you know this is the only universe? How do you know we are not walking in the midst of heaven right now? Did Jesus talk to Moses and Elijah high on the mountains? What is so different?"

"Okay, okay, Jim. You've got me convinced. I want to talk to my dad more than anything in the world. But I'm just not sure of all this. It's kind of scary, and I've heard people say"—I hesitated. "You're not supposed to talk to the dead."

"What is death, anyway? No life, no breath, no movement. I just told you we don't die. We will be more alive on the other side than here. In fact, we will not be weighed down by this heavy physical body. We will be free to come and go as we please. I believe what not talking to the dead means is not talking to someone who is dead inside. Someone who is weighed down with life and worries and has no faith. Someone who can't see, hear, or even care to understand anything but what is right in front of them. They're negative and dead inside. Do you understand what I'm trying to say? I could sit and talk to someone about God till I'm blue in the face, but if they're dead inside, they will never understand anything I say. Or even care.

"Some people are dead set on living their life the way they have been taught, and that's all right for them. They are dead to change.

It you don't believe in change, then you're dead to change. Unless they can be awoke on the inside and made whole, they will always stay dead to change.

"I think it's easier to awaken on the other side because we are not blinded by the physical aspects of the body, but don't quote me on that. I'm still learning," Jim continued.

"Marcie, I don't want to go too far into this. I don't want to confuse you. This has been a lot to digest for one day. So I got an idea." He winked and slapped his knees. "What do you say we take the boat out and drop a line for some fish and then come back here to cook? Then we can talk some more."

"That really sounds great. Let's do it." I was glad for the interruption of thought. It really was a lot to digest at one time. After all, it probably took Jim the whole twenty years to understand this himself, and he said he was still learning. *I sure don't expect to understand all this weird stuff in just one visit.*

In my mind I was still questioning it all. Maybe it was like he said: I was dead to the thought of ever talking to my dad. *But now I've been made whole in the idea of communication with my dad. Well, at least I'm on the way to being whole about this.*

To finally be able to talk to my dad about the farm and what's been going on in my life would be great.

"You ready?" asked Jim.

"Sure am. Let's get some fishing in."

Fishing was one of the things I most liked to do. It can be so calming to sit on a lake or river fishing, while the sun warms your back and the boat rocks you almost to sleep.

We made our way to his boat, which was tied to a tree. This was actually a little closer to his house than where I parked Bill's boat.

*Man, if Bill could hear all this, what would he think? Would he be one of the ones to say I'm crazy, or would he believe me and support what I'm doing?*

All the gear was in Jim's boat, and we were off. He said he knew the perfect spot for fishing, and he never went home empty-handed. It was the most comfortable feeling being in the boat with this kind but strange man of the swamps. *And on top of everything else, I've looked upon this man's face, and I'm not dead.* I had to smile. If the people in town only knew what a nice man he is. It's funny how people can come to conclusions about people just by looks or where they live. It's a known fact that in Cajun country people are judged by their last name. If for example your dad said all people with the last name of Bordelon were trash, then they were all trash. Just because of a last name. Go figure.

"Jim?" I asked. "You could pick any place to live. Why here?"

"I'm never bothered by anyone here. Of course it's probably because people are afraid of me. I've never seemed to fit any place but here. Also, I have some Indian heritage here."

"So you're some kind of recluse? Have you ever been married, or do you have kids?"

Jim's response was almost a whisper. "I was married once. But it just didn't work out."

"So you never had kids?"

"I did have one. She was beautiful. I guess she is in high school now."

"You don't sound like you're a part of their lives." I said.

"I had to make a choice a long time ago. Sometimes when two people start off on the same journey together, things happen. Instead of growing together, they grow apart. I wanted to grow more spiritually, and she didn't. The more time I spent away looking for what fulfilled me internally, it eventually put me on one path and her on another. I wanted to grow and mature spiritually, and she was stagnant and didn't care about spiritual things. She started to resent all the time I spent away either in research, church, temples, or what have you. She could have cared less about what I was doing, and it drove us further and further apart. She had a child to help her cope with her own insecurities and loneliness. Not that I didn't want my daughter—I did. But my soul yearned for fulfillment, and that's what broke us apart. It was as though we were together for a purpose, but our purpose was over. She went one way, and I went another."

I sat and listened to Jim as he continued.

"Marcie, we each have a journey. My journey brought me here. Your journey is your journey and is probably different than mine, but it's your journey. You can't bring everyone with you on this journey. Sometimes you will meet people on a similar journey. But no one's journey is exactly the same as anyone else's.

"You will find many, many people searching. All of them will search out what they feel is right. Most people will search in places that were taught to them growing up. If you were taught to go to the Catholic Church, then you will go to the Catholic Church. You will not search for anything else. We usually follow our ancestors. We follow the traditions of man. Most of us never break out that box.

"I, on the other hand, couldn't stop searching. I wouldn't settle for just one view. I wanted to know as many views as I could."

Jim threw out the anchor and started baiting his hook. I could see he was going to use a cane pole just like I did. To me that was the real sport of fishing. Use real worms and not artificial bait. Just like people who go camping in an RV, instead of in a tent or under the open skies. RVs? That's not camping. You have TV, air conditioning, a refrigerator, a stove. Real camping is roughing it and getting back to nature. Counting stars and fighting mosquitoes.

I picked up my pole and started baiting my hook. I noticed Jim was staring behind me. I laid my pole down and turned to see what he was looking at. There was a boat coming toward us.

It looked like T Boy's boat. There was someone else with him. It was Bill. *What in the world are they doing out here?* I felt like I'd just got caught with my hand in the cookie jar. What would they think of me with the swamp man?

T Boy's boat pulled up alongside of us. Bill spoke first.

"Hey, Marcie, been looking for you. I saw my boat tied off down a way back. What are you doing out here? You got a cow dropping a calf as we speak."

"Bill, T Boy, I'd like you to meet Jim." Jim nodded and kept on fishing. Bill said nice to meet you and T Boy just gave a crooked half smile.

"Okay, Bill, push over and let me sit next to you, and we can go. We can pick up your boat on the way back.

"Jim I really need to take care of business," I said as I got comfortable on the seat next to Bill.

Jim just nodded again. T Boy turned the boat around, and we went to pick up Bill's boat on the way back to the dock.

As I was getting into Bill's boat, he grabbed my hand. "Marcie, what were you doing with that man?"

"I wasn't doing anything. We were about to do some fishing."

"You know what I mean. Who was that?"

"His name is Jim."

"Please. Who was that, and what is your association with him?"

I pulled my hand back and jumped into Bill's boat. I turned and looked at Bill. He really looked concerned. "All right, Bill. His name is Jim Norman, and he is a new friend of mine."

"Where's he from?" Bill asked.

"He lives nearby."

"What do you know about this man? He could be a serial killer or something."

I smiled inside because that was exactly what I thought. "Bill, you are going to have trust me with this, please. I know what I'm doing. I'll see y'all later."

The motor started right up, and I was a gone pecan. I had taken off in Bill's boat before he had a chance to even think about getting in his own boat. I needed to get back to help the cows, and I sure didn't need twenty questions about what I was doing fishing with my new friend. The nerve of some people.

# CHAPTER 5

Soon I was back at the farm on my four-wheeler, going back and forth looking for any cows that were in distress. I had a couple of cows penned up at the barn, but they were not birthing at this time. I could hear the sound of another engine behind me. I saw Bill following at a distance, slowly getting closer, and he was pointing toward a clump of trees.

I headed that way, swerving in and out of some old oak trees. There behind another tree about ten feet in front of me was a cow. She was standing alone. I jumped from the four-wheeler and ran toward her. I just knew she was in trouble. I came closer, and there on the ground was a blob. As I walked closer I recognized a small calf. It wasn't moving. I knelt down next to the calf. It was too late. She was gone. She was still warm.

I felt a stabbing pain in my heart. *Oh, my God, I should have been here instead of traipsing in the woods at Jim's house. Maybe I could have prevented this.* Tears were running down my cheeks.

I stood up, and when I turned, I ran right into Bill. He caught me in his arms. I tried to break free, but he just pulled me closer, not letting me go. All I could do was cry. These last several weeks had really been trying. My emotions had been on edge from day one of the ghostly encounter. Now the guilt of not being here to help that poor calf was just too much.

Bill simply held me, stroking my hair. "It's okay. It couldn't be helped. It's okay; please don't cry."

The more he talked, the worse I felt. I cried even harder. I knew it was my fault. "My dad left me in charge of all this. It's my fault!" I cried.

"Marcie, look at me." I slowly raised my head to look in his eyes. If I didn't know better, I'd say he had tears in his eyes too. His hands slowly came up to cup my face. As his thumbs brushed the tears from my cheeks, he said, "It is not your fault. Please don't cry. It could have happened to anyone."

I couldn't believe how calming it felt in his arms. It felt like the most natural thing in the world to be in his arms. *It's funny—we've been friends so long, and I don't think we have ever hugged.* All of a sudden I could hear my dad in my head saying to not lose control. Toughen up.

I pushed away from Bill, wiped the tears from my eyes and walked past him to the four-wheeler. I grabbed an old pecan sack and came back to the calf. Bill started to grab for the bag, but I said, "I'll do that." I turned and looked at him as I yanked the bag closer to me. "You know you can't handle things like this. It will make you sick."

Bill's head hung a little, and he said, "You know, Marcie, you don't always have to be in control of everything. I'm here to help. I can help you, you know."

"I appreciate your concern, but I got it."

I threw the sack down and started to pick up the still warm dead calf. Bill knelt down and held the sack open while I slowly put the small, lifeless body of the calf inside it. It was a beautiful light brown with a white face and some white on each hoof. It was still a little damp from the birth. Again, tears welled in my eyes as I stood up. Bill stood with the sack in hand. He said, "I'll take this and bury it, okay?"

"Okay, Bill." I couldn't believe I'd said that. I turned to look at the cow, still standing there like she was lost or waiting for some response from her calf.

"Poor thing, it's like she is waiting for her baby," I said.

"Isn't this her first calf?" Bill asked.

"Yes, in fact it is," I said.

"She'll have plenty more," Bill responded.

"Sure she will," I mumbled.

He loaded the calf on the back of his four-wheeler and then turned to look at me.

I asked, "Were there any other problems you noticed?"

Bill said no.

"How did you know she was in trouble?" I asked. He knew some about raising cattle, but I didn't think he would know anything about this.

Bill said, "Well I had driven my four-wheeler over to visit with you. Your mom said she thought you might be in the pasture with the cows. That's when I saw that cow behind the tree. She seemed to be uneasy and kind of panting. That's when I started looking for you.

"T Boy just happened to be at the dock in his boat getting ready to head out to fish. I flagged him down when I saw my boat was gone. I knew it was either you or Frank in the boat. But Frank won't be back till Friday. So process of elimination, it had to be you. When I told T Boy I was looking for you and I thought you were in my boat, he was happy to bring me to look for you."

"Thanks for your help."

"You know I am always around if you need me. After all, we're best friends, right?"

"Yes, Bill, friends to the end." This was one of our sayings to each other. We always knew we were in good standing with each other as long as we acknowledged we were friends to the end.

We parted company, and I headed toward the barn to check on the situation. I checked each stall for any change in my cows. Everything was in order, and I started to head for the barn door when I ran into a wall of Old Spice. I stopped dead in my tracks.

"Daddy, is that you?" I asked. The scent was so strong. "Please, Daddy, say something." The scent slowly drifted away.

I tried to avoid my mom after what just happened. But to no avail.

"Marcie girl, is that you I hear?"

"Yes, Mom, I'm here."

"Bill was looking for you."

"I know; he found me."

I was hurrying to my room, but Mom called after me. "Marcie, was everything all right?"

I bit my lip and turned back. "No, Mom, it wasn't all right. Bill found me too late. One of the calves was dead."

"Oh Marcie girl, I'm sorry to hear that. But you know things like that happen. We have lost calves before."

"Yea, Okay, Mom, I'm headed to my room. I'm really tired."

"All right, sweetie. Have a good night."

That night sleep seemed to be a distant memory. Hours had passed when sleep finally caught up with me. In my dream I was standing on a beach. Then to my right I saw a man walking my way.

I got excited. *It's got to be my dad.* As he got closer, I realized it wasn't my dad. But there was something familiar about his walk. *It's Bill. Oh, my God, what is he doing in my dream?* He walked up to me with a smile on his face. He looked down at me and cupped my face in his hands, and I melted. He bent down and kissed me lightly on my lips. He then reached down and held me.

I woke up. I realized I was smiling and just had to scold myself for being so soft. I looked at the clock; 3:33 a.m. *Oh, it was just a dream. I'm safe.*

With a smile on my face I realized I really enjoyed that kiss. I could feel my heart beating fast and wondered, *Is this what it's like to kiss someone? My kiss at ten years old was nothing like this.* I turned over and went back to sleep.

I went right back into the dream. Again, I was standing on the sand looking out at the ocean, and Bill was by my side. Why, I don't know, but there he was. Off to my right, heading my way, was my dad.

"Daddy, here I am. I'm here. Daddy, it's so good to see you again."

"I see you brought a friend," Dad said with a smile on his face as he was looking over my shoulder.

I turned to see Bill smiling and putting his hand out to shake with my dad. "It's good to see you, sir," Bill said.

"It's good to see you too. I have to admit I'm a bit surprised to see you, Bill. Unless, of course, there has been some kind of connection between you and my daughter recently."

"Uh, yes sir, I—I love your daughter, and I want your permission to date her."

"Bill, what are you saying?" I demanded. "You know we are just friends."

"Marcie, listen. I have loved you from a distance since we were kids. I want an opportunity to show you how much I care." Bill's eyes were so soft as he looked at me.

Before I could say another word, Daddy said, "Bill, you have my permission to date my daughter."

I jerked my head around and yelled, "What? Daddy, you said never let my guard down. Not to get soft, and above all not to trust anyone."

"Marcie girl, I'm sorry for all the things I told you. I was wrong. The most important thing in the whole world is love. To love someone, you must trust; you must let your guard down."

Daddy's words were so sincere and loving, I knew it was true.

"Marcie girl, keep learning. Never give up on learning about love, learning truth. Just like you didn't believe I could come to you with a message. Also, you need to believe that life is not what you perceive. Life is not food and drink, houses and cars, cows and chickens. True life is within. It's loving your neighbor as yourself. I know you followed the light like I told you to. Now trust what is being said in this dream."

*Beep, beep, beep.* My eyes popped open. *Oh, my God, it's that damn alarm clock*. I reached over to turn it off. Then I sat up in the bed and cried. *Was that really my dad in the dream again? What was Bill doing there? I have to go tell Jim. I have to know if that was real or just a regular dream.*

I dressed quickly and started for the door.

"Marcie, where you off to in such a hurry?" Mom asked.

"I-I just got to go check the cows."

"Don't you want some breakfast?"

"No, Mom, I've got to hurry."

"Okay, sweetie, see you later."

I ran down to the dock like my pants were on fire. *Oh, my God, where's the boat? There's no boat at all. What will I do? I don't want to wait. I need to know if that dream was true.*

I paced back and forth wondering what to do. "Well, I guess I have no choice but to wait for the boat to come back. Why am I talking to myself again? I really need to stop that."

I walked back to the farm and got on my four-wheeler. I drove around checking on everything and nothing, just trying to stop thinking. I put out some hay and went back to start on my chores. Soon I was so busy that hours had passed before I knew it.

Then as I went around the barn, down the road I could see Jim headed my way. I ran toward him. "Oh, my God, I'm so glad to see you, Jim."

"Well, your dad said I need to get over here today."

"Jim, thanks for coming. Would you like to go sit under my favorite tree by the water?"

"Sure, that sounds great," Jim said.

We made our way down the road to my willow tree. "I just love this spot," I said. "It's a great thinking spot and just-be-lazy-day spot."

"I know what you mean, Marcie."

The sun was out, but I was thankful summer was not here yet. Everything was just beautiful today. The wildflowers were in bloom, and the bees were out. I could even smell the honeysuckle growing along the ground behind us.

"So Marcie, what's on your mind? Your dad said something to me about a dream. I didn't quite make it out."

"Are all dreams true, Jim?"

"No, sometimes your mind will bring up things from the day. I'm not a good dream interpreter," he said, "but go ahead and tell me about your dream."

As I went over the dream with him, I could see that he was really interested in what I was saying. It was like he was hanging intently on every word.

"You know, your dad was right, what he said about love."

"So it really was him?" I asked.

"You bet, girl, that was your dad. It's even confirmation that he sent me here to talk to you about it.

"Marcie, when you get a message from your loved one or even other heavenly entities, there will be confirmation, either in the physical or just an internal knowing in your spirit."

"What are heavenly entities?" I asked.

"Remember when I said you're never alone? I've learned over the years that we have a lot of heavenly help. Angels and Spirit guides, to name a few, are here to help us, to give us guidance and help when we need it, to push us in the right direction. I'm not sure, but I honestly believe we have different levels of heavenly help depending on our circumstances. God would never leave us on this planet alone. Marcie, you have the most bewildered look on your face." He had to laugh. "You look like you just saw a UFO." He continued to laugh. "Okay, just pick your jaw up off the ground."

"I'm sorry, Jim, these last several weeks since I heard my dad on the road, I feel like I have been in the Twilight Zone. It just doesn't seem real."

"Most people go through their whole life never experiencing anything like this. We talked about it yesterday. For many people, life just passes them by, and they have never lived or grown beyond what they were taught by Mom and Dad, school and church. Some people just don't think outside the box. Many people never grow, never learn that there is more to life than what you can see with two eyes.

"You also have to know, Marcie, that people are trained by others whom they look up to, never thinking for themselves. It's like they were programmed like robots: they believe only what they are programmed to know."

"Jim, you said something about learning. My dad said that too. He said to keep on learning."

"He was absolutely right. If you become stagnant or complacent, you will never grow. You must grow and reach for the sky, always searching, always learning, and always trying. Life is for living, not for being a dead body of water. Do you understand what I am saying?"

"I do. If I let myself stay stagnant and just keep believing what I've always believed was true and never open up to new things or new ideas other than what I've been taught, then I am not growing, right?"

"You got it, girl," Jim said with a smile on his face.

"Do you know why Bill was in my dream?"

"That's a good question. I'm not really sure. It could have been a part of your subconscious coming through in your dream. Or—" Jim paused.

"Or what?" I asked.

"Or it's possible he was there too."

"What? You can't mean that. How could he be sharing my dream with me?"

"Marcie, you have to think outside the box. Everything is possible. The only way you will ever know is to ask Bill for yourself."

"I couldn't do that," I said with my head down so Jim wouldn't see my face change four shades of red. I felt embarrassed to even be talking about that part of the dream.

"Well, speaking of Bill, here he comes."

I turned to see Bill walking our way. He waved and asked, "Hey, you two, what's going on?"

"Were just sitting here talking," I said.

"Good to see you again, Jim."

"The pleasure is mine," Jim replied. He slowly stood to his feet and shook off the grass from the back of his pants. "I need to get back," he said, straightening up.

As I was getting up too, Bill said, "You don't have to leave, Jim, on my account."

"I'm not. I just believe our talk is over." He winked at me and said, "At least for now."

Bill said, "Before you go, Jim, the boys want to get together and put some lines out Friday night. You know some night fishing. Would you like to join us?"

"That would great," Jim said as he looked at me. "Are you coming too, Marcie?"

Bill interrupted. "She's one of the boys; of course she's coming. You can't keep Marcie away from any kind of fishing."

I grinned and said, "I know that's right. Jim, would you like to meet us at about nine Friday night at the dock?"

"You got it," he said with a smile. "I'll see y'all then."

Bill moved a little closer to me as we both watched Jim walk away. Then he turned to look at me. I could feel my heart sink to my toes. *Oh, my God, what is he going to say?* Was he going to tell me he was in the dream last night?

Instead, he said, "So what is up with you two?"

I looked at him. "You mean me and Jim?"

"Yeah, you and Jim. What's up with you and that old man?"

"Jim is not an old man. He is just a very nice knowledgeable man of the world."

"He's probably thirty years older than you," Bill said.

"Bill, stop it!" I yelled. Then it came to me. I cocked my head at an angle and smiled at him. "You're jealous?"

"What? I'm not jealous; I'm just concerned about you getting involved with an old man like that."

"Bill, get this straight, because I'm not going to tell you again. I'm not involved with Jim. Do you hear me, Bill? He is just a friend. In fact, he knew my dad."

"Well, excuse me for caring." He ran his fingers through his hair. "Listen, I'll see you Friday, okay?" He sounded like a lost puppy.

"All right, I'll see you then," I said.

Bill walked a couple of steps and turned around. "Still friends?"

I smiled back at him. "Friends to the end."

# CHAPTER 6

The next couple of days went by fast. We had several calves that were born without any mishaps. Everything was going smooth. But I still had questions to ask Jim. *I'm still curious about the angels he was talking about.*

*Tonight should be interesting,* I thought. *Jim being such a loner, I hope he doesn't feel too uncomfortable with all of us.* "Of course he won't be uncomfortable. After all, he's a man of the world. A well traveled, wise man. He'll be fine." Again I was talking out loud. "I can't believe I'm talking to myself again. Really? Good thing no one hears me; they would wonder what's wrong with me."

Mom had fixed a great gumbo with chicken, sausage, big Gulf shore shrimp, and a big pot of rice for supper. She baked sweet potatoes and made a large green salad with one of her first tomatoes from the garden sliced into it. There was nothing like mashing a sweet potato, adding a little butter, and sprinkling some brown sugar on it. Yum. Mom liked to add her sweet potato to her gumbo instead of rice. Mom was the best cook ever. I ate till I was stuffed.

Mom was also in an unusually good mood. Not sure why, but she was just a-singing and humming as she started clearing up the dishes. "You have a great time tonight, sweetie," she said with a smile.

"Okay, Mom," I said. "Don't wait up."

"No, I totally overate, so I'll be in the bed by the time you make it to the dock tonight," Mom said.

*I haven't heard Mom hum or sing since Dad died. Wonder what happened to her?*

"Marcie, be careful tonight, and don't stay out late," she murmured.

*Something is definitely different about Mom. Normally she would be worried till I get home. I know her. She never falls asleep till I get home.* Mom was always a hard worker, and a definite worry wart, but today she seemed to be gliding through air.

The walk down the road to the dock was uneventful. It was funny, but a part of me wanted to run into my dad again. Another part of me was scared shitless and would be fine if I never ran into anything out of the ordinary, ever again.

I was caught off guard walking in the dark and almost ran into Bill. There was only one road to the dock that passed by my house. Most people parked up the road because the closer you get to the bayou, the worse the road was. It wasn't like some people didn't like to come mud riding out here, but Bill was funny about his truck. He kept it clean and tidy and in excellent running condition.

"Oh, hi, Bill. I didn't see you. It is pretty dark tonight." We both looked up into the sky at the same time to see the moon; it was nowhere to be found.

"Looks kinda cloudy," Bill said as he lowered his head to look at me and smile.

I paused and looked at Bill as though I had never seen him before. Bill really did have a wonderful smile. I felt a warmth ripple through my body, as if I'd just touched the electric fence running behind Dad's old barn. My heart started to beat faster. *What is wrong with me? This is Bill we are talking about, not Brad Pitt.*

We were the only ones at the dock. I looked down at my clock. It was almost nine o'clock in the evening. I climbed into the boat to hook up a battery-powered light. I could hear something in the water. I turned with light in hand to see an alligator submerging. Wow, he was awfully close to the boat.

I lived by water all my life and loved everything about it, but technically it was probably one of the most dangerous places in the world. Every tree might conceal an unsuspecting bear, bobcat, or critter of the night. The water was crawling with snakes, alligators, and some fish that would scare the pants off a city man. Not to mention all the bugs in the swamps. Leeches and wood spiders always make my skin crawl.

"I believe I see Jim coming," Bill announced.

I turned to see Jim's boat with a dim light pulling up from the shadows of the swamp. He pulled in beside me.

"Hi, Jim," I said with excitement.

About that time I heard T Boy walking up on us. "Hi, T Boy. You remember Jim, don't you?" I asked.

"I sho' do 'member dat man," T Boy said.

"I guess we can leave once Frank gets here," I announced.

"Oh, I forgot to tell you," Bill said. "Frank didn't come home this weekend. He said something about studying for some exams or something."

"How about we take my boat?" Jim asked.

"That would be fine," replied Bill. We grabbed our stuff and transferred to Jim's boat.

We'd gone a ways when Bill said, "I already have a couple of lines out. Let's check them first, rebait, and put out some more lines."

"Sounds good," I replied. I wondered when he had time to put lines out.

Bill must have known what I was thinking. He said he had been going out for about an hour each morning to set some lines and then checking close to dark and sometimes into the night. *So that's why the boat wasn't at the dock when I was headed to Jim's the other day.*

We pulled up to the first fishing line that Bill pointed out. T Boy was at the front of the boat and leaned over to pull up the line. Jim was maneuvering the boat right alongside the spot just like a pro. Bill was helping with the line, and I was putting on gloves to remove the fish. The bucket was ready, and there came the line.

"Get ready, Marcie," Bill said with excitement.

The line was up. "Not much to see," I said.

One mud cat on the whole line. *What's up with that?* I wondered. As T Boy held up the line, Bill rebaited about ten hooks. Then he turned and told Jim to go a little further down until he saw another red string in the tree up several feet to the right.

"Dar it be," T Boy pointed. Again, T Boy was leaning down to pull up the line. "Mais, there is sumting big on hea'." T Boy struggled to raise the line. Bill was trying to help; he bent down further and almost fell out of the boat. Jim and I both grabbed for Bill.

"I got it!" cried Bill.

As they pulled up the line, there was the biggest snapping turtle I'd ever seen on a line. "You just never know what you're gonna get out here," I said.

"Hurry, Marcie, cut the line," Bill yelled.

I reached over and cut the line with a pocket knife. It was like watching a trampoline bounce when the heavy turtle was released.

"You's got to watch fo' dose snappin' turtles. They get hold of ya hand and never let ya go."

Bill laughed, "You got that right, T Boy."

After checking several more lines and retrieving just a couple of small catfish, we rode further to a spot Jim said he had found. We put several more new lines out and baited them. It was going to be a slow ride back to the beginning. Running lines could take all night. You had to give the fish some time to find the bait. Some people waited hours and then rechecked their lines; some didn't come back till the next day to check.

All of a sudden the boat hit something in the water, and the motor stalled. We were jerked forward, throwing all of us onto the bottom of the wet boat.

"What the hell was that?" Bill yelled, trying to get up.

Each of us was scrambling up and resettling. My hand rested on the spotlight at the bottom of the boat, and as I started to stand, I raised the light and scanned the waters all around the boat.

"Look dar," T Boy said, pointing.

I moved the light to reveal the largest gator I'd seen in years. "Damn, that's a big gator," I said. "No wonder we didn't have much luck with the fish. This big boy probably ate them all."

Everyone laughed, but we all knew a gator could cause a fishing trip to be wasted, with no fish to bring home. We watched him head back around toward us, and as he got closer, he started to submerge.

*Oh, my God, he's going under the boat again.* I was stunned to see this huge alligator coming back to the boat. They usually go the other way. We all were intently watching as the alligator descended under the boat.

Bill turned to see me still standing up. "Marcie!" he yelled. He was reaching for me when the alligator hit the bottom of the boat, and I went flying off the side headfirst into the cold, dark water.

I came up gasping for air. I had dropped the spotlight, accidently torn from its battery pack, overboard into the murky water, and it had sunk like a stone. Then all of a sudden I felt the most awful pain in my arm yanking me back under the murky water. Fear gripped me so intensely that I couldn't even move. All I could feel was extreme pain in my arm up to my shoulder. Further and further we went. Down, down, down. My eyes strained to see anything that was familiar. I couldn't even see what had a hold of my arm, it was so dark.

My lungs were starting to spasm with pain. I needed air, and I needed it now. I tried to pull away when I realized I was being twirled like a rag doll. I was starting to lose consciousness. *Oh, my God, I'm going to die,* I thought.

I felt like my arm was being jerked and torn from my body. Then in the cold and dark, I could feel a yanking on my other arm. Then I felt myself pulled from the darkness. I drifted up in a peaceful movement that made me think I was lying on a cloud.

"Marcie girl, what are you doing here?" a familiar voice asked.

I opened my eyes. "Daddy, is that you? What's going on?" I was stunned.

"You're not supposed to be here," Dad announced.

"Dad? Where am I?" I looked around and saw the most beautiful sun shining. The trees were more vibrant than I had ever seen. It was so peaceful. "Is this another dream?"

"No, my little girl, you're with me," Dad said with his smile fading.

I turned and hugged him tight. I smiled and said, "Great!"

"No, Marcie you must go back. It's not your time," Dad said as he pushed me from him.

"But I want to stay," I cried.

"No, you must go; you have a wonderful life to live. You have grandchildren to have for your momma."

"No, Daddy, not me. You know I'm not getting married."

"You sure are getting married, Marcie girl, and I'll be right there by your side the day you do."

"Oh, Daddy, really?"

"Marcie, I will always be with you."

I felt myself falling to the ground. My body jumped as though I'd hit the ground like a ton of bricks. I was gasping for air and coughing up water. Bill was holding me across his lap. I looked up at him, and he grabbed me tightly. "Marcie, sweetheart, you're back." I could feel his body shake. He was wet and crying.

"Please, Bill, don't cry," I said, choking and gasping.

"Marcie, Marcie," he cried, holding me and rocking me in his arms.

I was too exhausted and confused to move. He held me for a while until he slowly stopped crying. He held me away and stared at me. "Marcie, I thought I had lost you forever," he said as he wiped the tears from his eyes. He started stroking my hair, again holding me tight.

It wasn't until then that I realized that the boat was at full speed. It was like I was just waking up. "Where is Daddy?" I asked.

"What? Your dad? He's not here, sweetheart," Bill said softly.

"But he was just here," I stated again.

Bill held me and rocked me and said, "It's okay now. I'm here."

As we pulled up to the dock, everyone was scrambling out of the boat like it was on fire, and that's when I realized that Bill was carrying me like a baby, as if I weighed nothing. What was all the fuss? I wondered.

"I can walk, Bill."

"No, ma'am, you are not walking," Bill declared.

"What's wrong?" I asked, dazed. "Why is everyone running? Why is everyone wet? Did you see my dad?"

"Marcie, we're going to the hospital." Bill carefully slid into the truck, still holding me. I looked around.

"Jim, you're here? I didn't know you could drive."

"I'm here, Marcie." Jim said.

"Did you see Daddy, Jim?"

"No, we were too busy getting you away from the alligator."

"What alligator?" I asked. I really was dazed. I was fighting to stay conscious.

Next thing I remembered were lights. What was I lying on? One light after another moved above me. I felt myself being pushed down a hall. All I could see were the lights on the ceiling. *What's all the hurry?* I could hear people scurrying all around, voices speaking.

A man in a white coat said, "Okay, little miss, we're going to take good care of you." I felt a small prick in my arm and drifted off to a peaceful sleep.

I woke in the quiet of the night. Was that a dream? What was going on? As I looked around, I didn't recognize anything. *Whose room is this?* As my eyes adjusted to the dark, I started to remember. *Oh, my God, there was an alligator. My arm!* I reached to feel if my arm was still there. *It's still there.* I sat up. Oh, my God my arm hurts. I could hear some breathing off to one side. I turned to see Bill, sound asleep in the chair next to the bed. I moaned when I moved my arm, trying to lie back down.

"Marcie," Bill said as he scrambled to my side. "You're awake? Go back to sleep, sweetheart. You need your rest."

"Bill, my arm."

"It's okay. Just go back to sleep." He reached over to cover me, and again I drifted off to sleep once more.

# CHAPTER 7

After several days of constant care from Bill at the hospital, with occasional visits from Mom, Frank, Jim, and T Boy, it was time to go home. I felt like the luckiest person in the world. Frank took off school to come visit, Jim left the swamps to visit, and T Boy found a way to visit from outside the hospital window of my room. Bill was like a doting dad the way he catered to my every moan. I'd never known anyone to care for me like that, and most of all I didn't lose my arm. It was only broken in two places, and my shoulder was dislocated. I had only a cast and some small stitches here and there.

I felt like all my shields were falling to the ground every day that passed. I was starting to feel ways I had never felt before. I thought my heart would explode with joy. Even the simplest of looks that Bill gave me had me catching my breath. His kindness and sincerity just melted my heart. *Oh, my God, it must be all the drugs they've given me. I'm feeling like a girl.* I had to smile at my own thoughts.

Mom showed up at the hospital door early one morning. "You ready, Marcie girl? I got you signed out, and we are ready to go. I pulled the car up to the front of the hospital. Bill, if you would go get her a wheelchair, I'll go get her stuff ready."

"Yes, ma'am," Bill said, walking out of the room with a smile on his face.

Mom gathered my things, smiling at me. She turned to see if Bill was out the door and then looked at me with a funny grin. "Marcie, that man loves you. He has been by your side the whole time. I also feel that he thinks it's his fault this happened to you."

"What? No, it was my own carelessness. Bill would never hurt me."

"I know that, Marcie, but does he know that?"

"I don't know, Mom, but I will talk to him."

Soon Bill was back with the wheelchair. He took my good arm to help me into the chair. Then Mom grabbed my stuff, and we were out the door. Bill again helped me into Mom's car as she put my stuff in the backseat.

She said, "Bill you're welcome to come by the house to visit, once Marcie gets settled in."

"I will be by soon to finish the chores." Bill had been going to the house early every day to do my chores for me, and somehow he always managed to be there when I woke each day in the hospital.

Mom got me settled in at home. It felt so good to be there. I had hardly gotten settled well when there was a knock on the door.

I started to get up, but Mom waved a hand and said, "You just sit there, I'll get it." I could hear a male voice at the door. Was it Bill already? Mom came in the room and said, "Marcie girl, you got company." There, trailing behind her, was Jim.

"Jim, it's good to see you," I said with a smile on my face.

"Marcie, you don't know how good it is to see you. We thought we'd lost you the other night."

"Come sit next to me; I have some questions. Would you please tell me exactly what happened? Things just seem kind of fuzzy."

"Well, do you remember anything from that night?"

"Only bits and pieces. I remember seeing the alligator coming toward the boat, and somehow I fell in the water. Then I had a terrible pain in my arm and was being dragged underwater. Then I saw my dad."

Mom walked in the room and asked if we wanted coffee. "Yes, that would be great. How about you, Jim?"

"Yes, thank you," Jim said with a nod to Mom.

"You said you saw your dad? Was he under the water with you?"

"No, that's silly. I was someplace where he was. He said I didn't belong there and that I had a life to live and grandkids to have for Mom."

"So you say you went someplace?" Jim looked puzzled.

"Jim, it was the most beautiful place I'd ever seen. It was so peaceful; I didn't want to come back. Why didn't you see Dad, Jim?"

"I didn't go anyplace like you did." When you fell in and the alligator grabbed you and dragged you under, T Boy and Bill were in the water right behind you. Honestly, I didn't think anyone was going to come up for air. T Boy had a huge knife in his hands when he went in. He tackled the alligator while Bill worked on getting you free. Can I tell you, I was sure worried. Y'all disappeared for what seemed forever. T Boy killed the gator, and Bill had you in his arms when they came back up. Bill did CPR on you till you started vomiting water and breathing again.

"Marcie, a lot of people don't get to go to the other side and come back and tell about it." He shook his head in amazement. "Did you say your dad told you, you were going to have kids?"

"Yes, can you believe it? I told him I wasn't getting married. But he said I was and he would be there. I must have knocked my head on something, because Dad would never say that."

Jim smiled. "Well, Marcie, you have to admit your young man is very taken with you."

"You're talking about Bill? Bill and I have been friends a long time."

"And?" Jim questioned with a tilt of his head and a smile.

"And we're friends," I said matter-of-factly.

"Don't kid yourself." He was smiling ear to ear. "I see the way the two of you look at each other. You have got to learn to trust."

"But Daddy said—"

Jim interrupted, "Marcie, trust is very important. You have to put yourself out there and trust. If you don't trust in love, you have nothing. You can't grow without letting your heart feel. You can't lock yourself up and throw away the key. Your dad loved you and your mom, didn't he?"

"Yes, he did. I believe he loved us both very much."

"There you go. Giving of yourself is very important. Look what you do for your mom. You give for her, don't you?"

I put my head down. "Yes, Jim, I guess I see what you're saying."

Mom walked in and brought us two cups of good strong coffee. "Wow, this coffee is good," I said as I smiled at Jim and Mom. "You know the hospital has the worst coffee ever. It was like drinking swamp water, and I got a firsthand taste of that.

"Mom, did I introduce you to Jim?"

"No, I don't believe you did."

"I met him several weeks ago. He is a good friend of mine."

"It's nice to meet you, Jim."

"It's a pleasure," Jim said. He turned to look at me. "You didn't tell me you had such a pretty mom."

I turned and looked at her. Mom pretty? I never thought of her as being pretty. She was just Mom. As I looked at her, I realized she was very attractive. She and I were the same height, five foot four inches of pure Cajun woman. She kept her brown hair pulled back and up in a twist to keep it out of her face. Her skin was milky white, and her eyes were big and brown. Out of the corner of my eye I saw Mom blushing with her head down, straightening her flowered shirt. It never occurred to me that Jim and my mom were close to the same age.

"Jim," Mom said, "my little Marcie girl is having a birthday soon, and I would like to invite you to come. It will be a small gathering with some of her closest friends."

"Mom, you don't have to go and prepare a party."

"I know I don't have to, but I want to."

"When will this be?" Jim asked.

"Let's give my little girl some time to recuperate, so I'll say in a couple of weeks."

"I will see you then," Jim replied.

Mom turned and left the room. Jim turned to look at me and said, "Your mom is very nice, and I'd be happy to come to your party."

I was surprised to see how much Jim was coming out of the woods to enjoy being with people again. I knew deep inside that this was hard for him, but I was totally happy to have any excuse to see Jim as much as possible.

"Thanks, Jim. Now you keep saying how important it is for me to learn to trust and love."

"Yes," Jim continued. "In all that I have learned over the years traveling from place to place, I have seen a common thread. And that common thread is love."

He took a sip of coffee, set the cup down, and continued. "You know, before you started this life and before you even came into this body of Marcie, you decided to have this life with these parents. We have known each other before this life. In fact, we may have known each other for many lifetimes. Most of us, not all of us, accomplish our mission here. If we don't finish our mission, we will come back again."

"What are you talking about, Jim? All of a sudden you have hit the ball in left field. You're not making any sense."

"I'm sorry, Marcie; let me explain. Everyone has their beliefs, and everyone has a right to believe as they wish. I hold nothing against any belief system. But it is my belief that we reincarnate. This belief is overlooked in the United States, even though I have found pockets of people who believe this concept. Other parts of the world have always believed this. I have gone many places and researched many books from around the world, and I have learned many things and have picked out truths according to the spirit inside me. If it agrees with my spirit, then it is what I believe. It's kind of like reading something a hundred times, but then one day you read it again, and it jumps out at you, and you understand it differently. Like a door of understanding has opened, and you get to glimpse a treasure that you never saw before.

"Of course I also believe that you, on your journey, may not come to understand all the things that I've learned in this lifetime. But the main thing I have learned was love. Love is very strong. It sees past all belief systems and cultures. It sees past all the unbelief in the world. Love surpasses everything. Do you know what I'm trying to say?"

"Well, Jim, sometimes I believe you've lost your mind with some of this stuff. But as far as what I can understand, you're saying all life is about, is love. It's about loving someone, even if they believe in reincarnation, UFOs, or Bigfoot and you don't," I said laughing. "Right?"

Jim slapped his knees and gave a hearty laugh. "That's it in a nutshell."

I had to wipe the laughing tears from my face. I looked at Jim and wondered. "Now tell me about how you know about reincarnation."

"Have you ever been hypnotized?" Jim asked.

I couldn't help but giggle. I thought to myself, *Let's see, between fishing and taking care of the farm, I squeezed in a session of hypnotism.* "No, Jim, you know I'm a simple country girl. Why would I need to be hypnotized, anyway?"

Jim smiled again and said, "Well, after my wife and I split up, I was having a lot of problems sleeping. I had a friend who was studying psychology, and he knew how to hypnotize. I asked him to help me so I could sleep again.

"I didn't want to take drugs to sleep. So he hypnotized me several times. It worked so well that we both decided to try some past life regression."

"Past what?" I asked.

"Past life regression is when you are hypnotized so far back that you surpass this lifetime and go to a previous lifetime. I can tell by the look on your face that this sounds crazy to you." He went on, "Anyway, we both had read about regression therapy, and we wanted to try it."

"One day he regressed me to my childhood. Then he went further, to another time and place in another body, and it just confirmed all the reincarnation I had learned about. Marcie, it's not imperative that you believe everything I say. God will show you what you need to know, when you're ready to hear it and not a moment before.

"Marcie, there is one thing I want you to remember, besides learning to love and trust; it is to have an open mind. In fact, without an open mind, you won't believe anything I say.

"There is so much I want to teach you, Marcie. In my heart, I believe that if I had to condense all the belief systems I have gone to and what my spirit inside says, I'd say it's all about loving so much that you lose yourself. Just like Bill and T Boy. They loved you so much that they didn't think twice about jumping in that water after you. They lost all fear, all of themselves, and just jumped.

"Everyone thinks this life is about them in a worldly way. Have you noticed how selfish people have gotten? They think about their house, their car, their job, their looks, and they forget this world is not about them, it's about us. It's turning into an 'I' generation. When you can love someone so much that you don't think of yourself, then you have reached perfection. Jesus laid His life down for the world. He knew the power of love and how to use it. When you can love someone, even when they have nailed you to the cross, or if someone comes in your house and kills your family, but you can still look that person in the eyes and forgive them, you have reached perfection. When you learn to love so much that you don't judge others, you have reached perfection. I believe that means you have become Christ-like. A part of Bill and T Boy became Christ-like that night. I honestly believe that is what life is all about. We come here to conquer this body and see past the physical to the spiritual and in my opinion the spiritual is nothing but Love with a capital *L*.

"Marcie, I honestly believe that is what your dad has been trying to tell you lately. I know when he was here he taught you not to trust, not to get hurt, to keep to yourself and become self-sufficient. He was trying to protect you from hurt, but people will always hurt you. Try to see past the hurt and accept love anyway. Go ahead—let your guard down, get married and have your family, and learn to give from love. You will know what I am talking about when you have kids. You love them so much, you would lay your life down for them."

"Wow, Jim, I didn't think you could talk that much," I said with a crooked smile.

"I'm sorry, I just get so passionate about this subject. Remember: my life is what it is today because I've wanted to learn what I could on this subject.

"Listen, I have bent your ear long enough. Let me get out of here so you can rest." Jim got up and said, "Welcome back."

"Don't be a stranger, Jim. Come back and see us again."

Jim turned and saw my mom coming back into the room. He looked at me and said, "You bet I'll be back."

Mom said her good-byes and came back into the living room. She picked up the newspaper and started thumbing through the pages. She slowly lowered the paper. She looked at me. "Marcie, how long did you say you have known Jim?"

"I met him several weeks ago, I guess. Why?"

"He seems very knowledgeable about life. I didn't mean to eavesdrop, but he caught my attention with some of the things he said."

"Mom, are you okay with what Jim said?"

"Absolutely," Mom said.

"Really, I thought you would think all this stuff strange."

"Well, Marcie girl, I didn't say it wasn't strange and unusual. But I believe I've seen your dad and talked to him."

"What?" I yelled, almost choking on my coffee. "I can't believe it. You too?"

Mom started to laugh. Then I started to laugh.

She wiped the cheerful tears from her face and said, "I saw your dad, and he told me he would always love me but to stop mourning him and not to let anything hold me back from loving again. He also said I had a good life ahead. Once he told me all that, I felt a weight lift off me. I knew he was okay."

That must have been when I noticed a change in Mom. "I hadn't heard you sing in long time. It was good to see you happy again."

"Thanks to your dad, I feel I got my life back," she said with a smile. "Don't get me wrong, Marcie, I will always miss your dad, and no one could ever take his place."

"I know, Mom, I know."

"So you saw him too?" she asked.

"Yes. He told me almost the same thing. He said I was going to get married and have grandkids for you." Again we started to laugh. It was just wonderful to be able to open up with my mom about this. It was also confirmation. Mom and I had seen and heard Daddy. It was good to know he was watching over us and not dead in a casket under the ground and that life does go on. I will always miss seeing him, but it's good to know that his essence will always be here with us.

"Marcie, I want to apologize about the other night when you said you saw your dad in a dream." Mom paused. "I didn't believe you."

"It's okay, Mom; I understand."

Mom and I talked into the wee hours of the night. I told her about everything. She heard me. She really heard me. I'm not sure we had ever talked like this before. But it sure felt good to connect with her like that. Also, it seemed that every time Jim and I had our little lessons, he left me with things to think about. Some of this was really hard to swallow. But I guess like Jim said, whenever I'm ready God, will make a way for me to know what I need to know, when it's the right time.

# CHAPTER 8

The next couple of weeks were a bit hectic, since Mom was planning a party that I didn't even want. I just couldn't break her heart, so I went along with it the best I could.

Bill was still coming over to try to help me. I knew I was giving him a hard time about helping me, but people don't change overnight. Bill would tell me, "You know I'm just trying to help, but you are hardheaded and ornery."

My reply was always "I know. I'm just not used to anyone helping me." I always saw the disappointment in his eyes, which seemed to pull at my heart like never before. To make him smile, I would quote our favorite saying, "Bill, we still friends?"

"Friends to the end," he said with a smile that warmed my heart.

Mom made arrangements at the Knights of Columbus Hall to have my birthday party. Even though I continued to oppose this party, she acted like a dog running with a stolen hot dog. She just ran with it, never hearing a word I said.

I begged and pleaded with her not to invite the whole town, just have my close friends. Of course my close friends I could count on one hand. Mom continued to tell me that she did not invite the whole town; she only invited some friends. Now, why would you rent a hall for just a small amount of people? Her excuse for using the hall was because she didn't want every Tom, Dick, and Boudreaux running wild in her house.

The party was planned for Saturday night. According to the TV we had a storm headed our way, and it could end up being one of the worst we'd had all season.

"Mom, we really need to postpone this party. People wouldn't be caught dead running around in a storm like this." I insisted.

"Marcie girl, it won't be here by the time we have your party. We'll be long gone before it hits."

"Well okay, Mom, I guess you know best," I said, biting my lip. There was just something about this party that didn't sit right. I didn't know if it was because I didn't want all the attention or if there was something deep down inside that said this was not going to be a good night.

Mom was at least partly good on her word. Not only my closest friends came but some people from town, and I think my whole graduating class arrived en masse to my party.

Frank came with a female acquaintance from college. Bill was there, of course, and Jim came with a smile and the wisdom of the ages in his eyes.

Then from the side of the room I saw T Boy walking up to me with a mile-wide smile on his face.

"Hi, T Boy, I'm real glad to see you." He just stood there smiling at me. "What?" He looked down. I followed his gaze to the floor. To my surprise he was wearing boots. "Oh, my God, T Boy, is that alligator boots?"

"It sho' is. It be your alligator," he said with pride. "Mais, I had me a awful time finding and getting me dat gator to the house. I then cleaned him up real good and sent off the skin to make me some boots. Dat damn alligator will be under my foot forever." We both laughed like there was no tomorrow.

"T Boy, I want to thank you for helping me that night."

"Cher, I would give my life for you," he said.

My heart felt like it would explode from the sincerity of his words. I knew he meant what he said. I reached up on my tiptoes and gave him a big hug.

The party was getting under way with a good head count of about twenty from town. There was even a band. It wasn't much of a band but it was music. They played a little country music and my favorite zydeco. At least I guess that's what all that noise was. Sometimes they would hit a note so out of tune that it sounded like a squealing pig. But the music did liven up the place.

We also had a lot of good food. Mom made sure all the Cajun cuisine was present. There was some fried shrimp, fries, coleslaw, cracklin's, boudin, and one of T Boy's specialties, fried alligator. Come to find out this alligator was the one and only alligator that tried to eat me. *How funny; now we are eating him.* T Boy went back that night to get that gator not only for the skin but also for the meat. You don't waste food in the swamps. If you kill it, you're eating it.

My three-tier birthday cake was beautiful, with little yellow flowers circling every layer, and there were balloons galore all throughout the hall.

After a while I noticed we had a latecomer walk in. When she opened the door it flew out of her hand. The wind had picked up so much that it looked like her clothes and hair were going to be ripped right off of her. She struggled to get in and keep her wits about her.

She was one of my classmates from school. I greeted her at the door. "Mary Ann, are you okay?"

"The wind is really picking up out there," she said.

"I know, we have a storm coming."

"Well, I think it's here," she said with a sigh.

"Glad you made it. Go and get you a drink at the bar, and have a good time."

Mary Ann and I were not that close, and I hadn't seen her since school. I soon saw that she was really there to do more harm than good.

As the party went on I noticed that she was hanging around Bill a lot. *If I didn't know better, I would think she was flirting with him.* Bill was laughing and seemed to enjoy the attention. As I was talking with some of my friends, I could see her edging closer and closer to him. Every so often she would look my way to see if I was watching. Why was she tormenting me this way? It was like she was purposely flirting with Bill to get under my skin.

Mom was watching me watch Mary Ann. I heard Mom clear her throat behind me and I turned to look at her. She said, "Kind of looks like Bill has got the attention of that pretty girl over there."

"Well, it's a free country. If he wants to make of fool of himself, that's up to him." I jumped up to go get something to drink. I could feel heat rising in my face.

*Bill is totally oblivious of what that girl is doing*, I thought. *He hasn't even noticed me tonight. What an idiot to just let that girl flirt with him.* I was fuming. I wondered if smoke was coming out from under my collar, I was so mad.

I stomped back to where I was sitting. I decided after a while to ignore all this hogwash and go talk to Jim. Jim took one look at me and knew exactly what was going on. How, I'll never know. But sometimes I swear that man is psychic or something.

Jim put his hand on my arm and said, "Just calm down, Marcie. You know Bill's heart is only for you."

"No, I don't know that. We have never had a contract between us. He is free to do as he will."

"You have to know that problems come into our lives all the time. But the secret is not to let the problem control you."

"What problem, Jim? Bill's free, and so am I." I was looking daggers at Jim.

"Please listen to me," Jim said gently. "You can't ignore the problem, because it will not go away."

"So what?" I snapped.

"You must confront the problem head on."

"What problem? I have no problem," I said, slamming my hand down on the table.

"Marcie, I see the way you look at Bill. I know you love him."

I slowly turned my head toward Jim with a questioning look. "How do you do that, Jim? How did you know?"

"It's pretty obvious," Jim said with a smile.

"If you can see that, then everyone else can see it too," I said with my head down. "That means I've turned into a girl since Dad died."

He grinned. "Well, it's a good thing to be a girl when you are one. You can't keep to yourself the rest of your life and never love." Jim's face had this pleading look.

"But—"

"Marcie, there are no buts. Admit to yourself right now that you love Bill. I can see that you are fuming with jealousy. You must love your way through this situation," he pleaded.

"Love? You got to be kidding. Look what happens when you open your heart and think you love someone. You get tormented," I said as my face grew redder and redder.

"You must love that girl and love Bill."

"What do you mean? Sometimes I think you get your information from outer space. You just don't make any sense."

"It looks to me as if your friend from school is trying her best to steal Bill from you, either because she wants him or because she wants to hurt you. I'm not sure what her motive is. But you must stop this before it gets out of hand."

"How, Jim?"

"Always in love," he said quietly. "You have to know that nothing happens in this life unless it's meant to be. Jealousy is a bad vibe, very negative. You must not let it get a hold of you. You must counteract it with positive. Do you know what I mean?"

"No, not exactly," I said softly.

"Go over there with your head up. Go and be as kind as you can. Love covers a multitude of sins. Love your neighbor. Love that girl."

"Jim, I don't know if I can. All I want to do is go over and slap her into next week."

"Marcie, you are one of the strongest people I have ever met. You can overcome this desire to go slap her face clean off her head."

With that comment I started to laugh. It sounded so funny when he said it.

Jim laughed too. "Now don't you feel better?"

"Yes, I do," I said, smiling.

"Laughter is a very positive vibe, and it destroys the negative. Positive always covers the negative, just like the light always covers the darkness."

"I have a question, Jim."

"What's on your mind?"

"You said nothing happens unless it's meant to happen."

"Yes, that's right," he said.

"Are you telling me that even this terrible situation is meant to be?"

"Absolutely," Jim said. "You are seeing this situation all wrong. You see it as something bad, and I see it as an opportunity."

"You have lost your mind, Jim. The only opportunity I see is the chance of being on the Channel 5 news after I turn this party upside down."

Jim laughed. "This is just another opportunity for the Universe to show you yet another lesson in love. A couple of weeks ago you learned a lesson, and now it's time for another one. And I have to tell you, once the lessons start, they don't stop until you finally get what love is all about. I can bet you that you are in for a long, long time of training.

"Look outside, Marcie." I turned and looked out the window. "See how the trees bend from the wind?"

"Yes," I said.

"Only the weak trees and limbs will fall."

"So what are you saying?"

"You know that saying, what doesn't kill you makes you stronger?"

"Yeah, so what?"

He looked intently at me. "Think about it, Marcie."

"I guess what you're saying is, we all go through tough times and the tough times make us stronger," I said, already exasperated with the conversation.

"You've got it, girl." Jim beamed with pride. "Going through these lessons is not easy, but you will learn all you need to learn from them. You will be wiser and stronger. You'll see.

"God never makes a mistake. If you give in to the negative, no matter what it is, you have not conquered the negative, and if you don't conquer this mountain, you will most definitely have to go around it again.

"The good thing is that if you fall, you can pick yourself right up and try again."

"Okay, Jim, I get it. But how does 'love' play into this?"

"When you deal with people, you must lose your desires to hurt someone who is hurting you. If you love Bill, you will show him that you care and then put the ball in his court. When you give love in return for bad, it gives you an upper hand in the spiritual realm. It's like it paves the way for miracles to happen in your life.

"Don't get me wrong, Marcie. Fight for Bill, but if his choice is that other young lady, you will hold your head up high and show love the whole time. You will not let the evil win.

"There are no mistakes. If Bill is for you, he will be for you and no one else.

"God is in complete control of our lives, if our heart is in the right place. What looks like disaster is really a blessing in disguise. What I have learned is that even if I make a wrong choice by trying to do right, it always brings me back around to where I am supposed to be in life.

"So all you do, girl, is walk over there. Be pleasant and loving. Then walk away. It won't be long, and you will see how love works. So go."

I got up, threw my hair back, and slowly walked over to Mary Ann sitting at the bar next to Bill. "Hi," I said softly. I looked her in the eyes and thanked her for coming. I told her it showed me how much she cared for me that she would weather the storm for me. I then leaned down and kissed her on the forehead. When I looked at Bill, his mouth was open in disbelief. I stepped toward him, gave him a big hug, and thanked him also for putting in so much effort to make this day special for me. When I turned to walk away, I felt eyes on my back. I knew I had made an impression.

I could see Jim watching the whole thing from a distance, and I smiled as I got closer to him. When I sat back down in my chair, he said, "Way to go, girl."

Jim was right; about ten minutes later, I saw Mary Ann get up and leave the party. Next thing I knew, Bill was by my side. I looked him straight in the eyes and asked, "Still friends?"

"Friends to the end," Bill said with a grin. "So Marcie, you want to dance?"

I looked at Jim and he winked at me and nodded. I turned to Bill and said, "Sure, I'd love to."

He led me by the hand to the middle of the floor and swung me into his arms like he meant it. It took my breath away. I felt myself just melt into his arms. "I don't think we have ever danced before," I said nervously.

"No, I believe you're right; I think I would have remembered that." He had a funny grin on his face.

As he held me even closer, I just couldn't believe all the emotions going on inside me. He smelled so good, and I just realized how dressed up he was. *I've never felt like this before. I wonder if this is what love feels like.* Still in my mind I could hear my dad preaching not to let my guard down. How do I fight the dad that raised me and the dad I saw in my dreams, whose philosophy was so different? Part of me wanted to run away, and another part of me just wanted to keep on melting into Bill's arms until you couldn't tell where one of us began and the other ended.

"Marcie, sweetheart?" Bill said softly in my ear. I looked up at him. "I—I want to tell you something."

"What is it, Bill? You okay?"

"I just, just wanted to say, I … uh, happy birthday."

"Thank you, Bill. I owe it all to you and Mom."

He squeezed me a little more, and I winced from my arm. "I'm sorry, I forgot all about your arm. Is it hurting you a lot?"

"No, actually it's doing pretty good. Bill, you do know it was all my fault that I was standing up in the boat that night. I take full responsibility for my awkwardness and falling in the water."

"No, Marcie, it was my fault for not taking care of you. Any time we ever went out to the swamps growing up, your dad would always tell me to watch over you and keep you safe."

"You're kidding," I said. "I didn't know that. But Bill, I'm a grown-up now. It's okay."

"Marcie, I will always watch over you," Bill said.

"Okay, how about I try to be more careful, and you just keep watch?"

His head rolled back with one of the heartiest laughs I had ever heard from him. It made me giggle too, to see the amusement in his face.

"You look real nice tonight, Marcie. I didn't know you had legs," Bill said with a grin as he held me at arm's length and looked down at them.

"Well, you better take a good look mister," I said with a crooked smile, "because you'll probably never see me in a dress again."

"I know, and I'll never see you in pink rubber boots either," Bill teased, and we laughed.

Actually, it was the only dress I owned because there was no place on a farm for a dress. "If it hadn't been for Mom, I sure wouldn't be wearing one now." I said.

"Marcie, there you go again." Bill tilted his head to the side with his eyebrow cocked up.

I felt my face turn four shades of red. "You know what I mean. Stop messing around." I buried my head in his shoulder and smiled.

Then he stopped dead in his tracks. I looked up and saw him gazing behind me toward the door. I turned to see what he was looking at, and there was Mary Ann coming in the door hand in hand with T Boy. The wind was still howling outside, and it looked like we all could be blown away at any time.

Bill and I both watched T Boy escort Mary Ann to the dance floor and start dancing. I looked at Bill. "Did you know that T Boy could dance?"

He smiled at me and said, "No, who would have thought he knew how? I've never even seen him look at a girl either." We started to laugh at the thought of T Boy in his new alligator boots dancing with Mary Ann.

As we continued to dance I looked just past Bill's shoulder in the corner. There was my dad just standing there smiling. "Daddy?"

"What?" Bill asked.

"I was just thinking of my dad."

"You know, Marcie, it's kind of funny you mentioned him tonight, because I had a dream about him the other night."

"What!" I exclaimed. I stopped dancing, looked at him, and asked what happened in the dream.

"Well, Bill said, you were there, and your dad came walking over. I had the opportunity to ask him if I could date you."

"You what?" I said, starting to shake.

"He gave me permission to date you." I looked again in the corner and saw my dad wink at me.

"Well?" Bill asked.

"Well, what?" I asked remembering the dream.

"Well, will you go out with me? You know, like a real date. I'm not talking about fishing or hunting or frogging. I'm talking about going with me to dinner some time or to a movie. So will you go with me?"

Silence filled the air. I think I paused too long, because when I looked at him he was starting to hang his head in disappointment. I felt a stab in my heart. "Of course I'll go out with you, Bill." His head rose, and he smiled. He grabbed me up and swung me in circles. "Put me down Bill before I change my mind." We both laughed.

*One day I really need to tell Bill that I had the same dream.* I looked again, but Dad was gone. Then I turned to look at Jim. I could tell by the look on his face that he had seen everything. What a surprising night this turned out to be.

Just then the door flew open with a bang, and one of the townspeople, Hank the mechanic, came running into the party. He ran in and hesitated, searching the room till he saw Bill. He ran up to him, grabbed him by the shoulder, and said, "Your mom has asked me to find you."

"What is it?" Bill demanded. "What is it?"

"Your dad never made it back from fishing. She said you need to get some help and go find him." Bill was already halfway out the door before Hank finished his sentence.

The music stopped, and T Boy, Frank, and some other men from the town ran up to ask Hank what was going on. I ran for the door after Bill as Hank explained the situation to the others. I ran out into the rain and wind, and my dress went flying up to my waist. As I tried to get control of my dress, my hair, and my composure, I noticed Bill getting in his truck to leave. He turned around and ran back to me.

"Marcie, go on inside. I'll be back later."

"No, Bill, I'm coming with you."

"No, you're not," he yelled to be heard over the storm. "Do what I say!" Then he pulled me to him and kissed me hard on the mouth. "Now go back inside."

He turned and ran back to his red four-wheel-drive truck, He jumped in and sped off, fishtailing and almost hitting another parked truck.

About that time the men came flying out the door. I ran up to T Boy. "I'm coming with you."

"No, dat's no place for you. You go back inside dar and tell everyone what be going on. It will be okay; I will keep an eye on ya man."

I ran into the hall and went to Mom. I told her what was happening. I told her I was going to the dock to find a boat to help. Then I got slapped down again.

"No," she yelled, "you are not going. I lost your dad, and then I almost lost you to that gator. I cannot bear to go through that again. Please promise me you won't go. Please, Marcie girl, please!"

I couldn't stand to see the pain and fear in her face. "Okay, Mom, I won't go."

I was so frustrated that I couldn't go out with the boys and help. Being a girl sucks. When things get hard they don't look at me like one of the guys anymore; they just treat me like a small, weak girl.

"Let's go home, Marcie. It kind of looks like the party is over anyway," Mom said with a disappointed look on her face. More than half the people were gone, and the storm seemed to be getting worse. We never even got to cut the cake.

# CHAPTER 9

It proved to be a long night. After loading up the car with the uneaten food and cake, we picked up and then headed for home.

On our way, we stopped by to see Bill's mom, but she had so many people there that we slipped out the side door after we paid our respects.

We settled down at home drinking coffee and talking of the night. Jim had come by for a while but couldn't stand just sitting around, so he left.

After changing into more appropriate clothes, I made several trips to the boat dock, wind and all, with a promise to Mom not to venture any further. It would be a miracle if all the boats out there didn't get tossed onto the banks. As I sat nervously in the living room, I heard some noise outside. *Bill*, I thought as I jumped from my seat to open the front door and see what all the racket was. It was several trucks headed toward town. "They must have found him," I told Mom.

I saw Jim walking toward me. I ran out to meet him. The wind seemed to be blowing everything not nailed down.

"Marcie, they found Bill's dad," Jim said loudly over the constant wind. "He was holed up on the bank under his raincoat."

"That's great. I know Bill must be relieved he found him."

Jim gave me a serious look. "We haven't heard from Bill yet."

"What? I thought he found his dad."

"No, you know that bloodhound, T Boy? He found him. But don't panic, girl, I'm sure Bill is fine. He'll be in before you know it."

I knew I should have gone with him. He never should have left alone. What was he thinking? What was I thinking for backing down like a girl and not going with him? We weren't thinking at all, that's it. Someone was in trouble, and we jumped.

Jim and I walked back to the house as the rain started again. "Jim, I'm going crazy here. What do I do?"

"You can only let it go."

"Let it go? Are you crazy? Bill is out there in this storm, and you want me to let it go?"

"Marcie, the more you let go and let God do His thing, the better things get."

"Do you mean don't worry?" I asked.

"No, but don't let it consume you. Just like at the party. Just thank God that Bill is okay and will be here soon. Then let it go. Go wash dishes or take a shower, but don't just sit here worrying that he is not coming home."

"But what if he doesn't come home?" A tear ran down my check, and I turned away so Jim couldn't see.

"Marcie, life is only as hard as you make it. If God took him tonight, you can't change that. So let it go. Be as positive as you can, but know that God always has your best interest at heart.

"This holds true for all things. If it was your health we were talking about, it would be the same thing. Always trust God that He knows what He is doing in your life. Everything, Marcie, everything is for a reason. Just because it seems bad doesn't mean it is. Losing my family seemed like the most awful thing in the world to me, but look at the knowledge I have gained. When I think of all I learned on my journey and how I have the opportunity to help you because I've lived it—"

Jim smiled as he realized Marcie was learning yet another lesson from God. "Stop trying to control this situation. Give it to God.

"Listen, I know I've said this before, but when you give of yourself above your own desires, like giving the situation over to God to handle instead of you; when you lay your life down for a friend, the way T Boy and Bill did for you; when you love those who persecute you like at the party with Mary Ann; when you say, 'Forgive them, Father, for they know not what they do,' like Jesus did—then and only then can you feel pure joy. This is what makes your spirit grow. This is laying up treasures in heaven. You learn that life is about giving, not taking. We are all one, Marcie. When you do for one, you do for all. The great Master, Jesus, knew that."

"I think I know what you're saying, Jim. But I have never heard this before."

"Of course you have, Marcie."

"When have I ever heard this?"

"Every time you went to Sunday school or church and heard of the love of God, you read the Bible, every time you let your heart act over your own desire, you were learning truth. Look how Mother Theresa gave her life to serve others. Every time you heard stories like this, you heard this message. When a mother has a child, she gives her life for that child.

"We have talked about this before. In fact, you will notice that I will repeat myself often to get my point across. I will tell you what I know until it is embedded in your consciousness. Now, tell me you've never heard this?"

"I guess I have, but I never understood it like you're explaining it to me now. So I guess you're telling me to trust God all the time, and love is above the rest."

"Yes, trust God to know what is going on, and know He is in control. I'm not saying that if Bill doesn't show up by the time this storm has calmed, we won't go looking for him. But worry won't change a thing. Love God enough to let Him be in control. Tonight you learned to let go of jealousy and let love do its magic. Right?"

"Yeah, I guess. Now I need to let fear go and trust God to know what is right in this situation."

"Marcie, I got my foundation in church, but I feel there is more to learn than just in some denomination. The world is a smorgasbord of learning opportunities. Now, don't take this wrongly, but what I'm about to discuss with you is my opinion, okay? I've learned a lot in my journey, and I feel that church is meant only to lay a foundation for us. Church is a stepping-stone. The true nature of God is to be learned from living life, making mistakes, meditation, and listening to that still small voice that never steers you wrong. Just learn to listen to the right voice. God was expressed through Jesus, and now God is meant to be expressed through us. We are writing the word of God all the time. God is infinite, and learning about Him is infinite. Now you know why I stay in the woods to myself," Jim said.

"Honestly no, I really don't understand why you seclude yourself from others. You should be teaching this to people."

"I am, Marcie." Jim smiled. "You're my first pupil.

"Marcie, in my opinion people don't want to hear that the kingdom of God is within and that everyone can reach this kingdom without an organized religion. It's not about the physical; it's about the Spirit of God within. Don't get me wrong. I still believe a good church is a good, basic foundation. But don't let them totally influence you.

"What I've noticed about some denominations is that they will take one or two Scriptures and base a whole religion on them, instead of seeing the whole picture. It's like concentrating on the period without reading the sentence. Did you ever wonder why we have so many religions? Look at the divisions in the church. There shouldn't be any division with God's people. How can we all come together in love when we are squabbling about which religion is right or wrong? This war has gone on for centuries and has caused more death and destruction than anything.

"Most people don't see past the physical aspects of life to a richer and more powerful presence within. If you believe differently, people will call you crazy and say you're practicing black magic. Some people are worse than others. They will judge you because you listen to 'a voice' instead of listening to the priest or pastor. Most religious people interpret the Word of God in a black-and-white Moses mind-set."

"What are you talking about, Jim? I've never heard of this 'Moses mind-set' you're talking about." I tilted my head slightly, hoping to hear better.

"Moses introduced the law. You know, 'Thou shalt not do this or that.' But Jesus brought grace. God knew we could never be perfect by obeying all the laws. In fact, people have taken the Law and made themselves judge and jury. But Jesus came to show a new way of life, a new covenant, a covenant of love—a covenant of grace.

"Anyway, most religions mix the law and grace together. We are only under the grace of God. The Great Master knew this and taught this through His ministry on earth. In fact, I believe He is still teaching us from the spirit world today. He teaches us by His spirit.

"I have come across a small percent of the people that have broken away from the traditional ways and have sought the Spirit of God. Most people don't know they have been set free from the law. The only law we are under is love. The Scriptures say the fulfillment of the Law is love. That is why I always talk about love.

"Everyone has the potential to reach the God Spirit inside, and just because they haven't yet doesn't mean we should think any less of them. Every second of every day is a learning process."

"Jim, you make this sound so simple."

"Once you get the concept, it's simpler than you know. But it is hard to do."

"How hard can love be?" Then I realized I was failing miserably in love. "Never mind, Jim, I see how hard it is," I said with much regret.

"Don't feel bad, Marcie. People find it hard to release their own desires and wants to give enough to love. If love is done in the right way it can heal a nation. But the wrong concepts of love can destroy a nation. Selfless love is the only answer. You know the phrase, 'What would Jesus do?'"

"Yes," I said.

"Well—" Jim paused. "What would Jesus do? Would Jesus judge anyone for anything? He saw the heart of man. Past their flaws, past their inability to love completely, past their human desires. He loved completely. All He wanted was to reach people from a deeper standpoint to show them they are more than what they think they are.

"The apostles were not perfect, but He loved them anyway. Did He judge them for their inabilities to be perfect? Judgment is in the eye of people because they see nothing as perfect. But God is perfect, and everything He created is perfect.

"People see in a human aspect and will never be happy. But once we've really touched the inner realm, the kingdom of God, the chi, the power within, the core, and feel the perfection within, which is God, then and only then will we learn not to judge. People judge by what they see, hear, and think. But the Spirit of God is perfect and judges no one. This God Spirit is in everyone, but most of us haven't found this yet."

"Jim, I really enjoy listening to all the things you have to say. Is it what my dad was trying to tell me about?"

"You bet it is. I believe that when your dad died and he felt the peace and love of the Universe, he knew he'd been wrong all those years here, and he just wants you to know what he has learned and more."

"Wow, how can there be more?"

"Remember what I said. Your learning is infinite. How could anyone ever know God completely? So why would we only settle for what little we learn in this life, from other people's perspectives? Why settle for just a taste when you can have a meal?"

I got up and hugged Jim's neck. "Thank you so much for being here with me tonight and all your comforting words."

He smiled and said, "Now let's go see what the weather is doing." We walked outside to see that the rain had stopped and the wind had dropped considerably. Jim turned to face me, grabbed my shoulders, looked me straight in the eyes, and said, "Now, young lady, let's go find your beau."

Jim always had this way of making me feel that we could conquer the world, and tonight I needed that.

# CHAPTER 10

Jim and I were headed to the dock on the old rutted dirt road where I'd had my first ghostly encounter with my dad when I had that feeling again.

"Jim, it feels like someone is here." He stopped dead in his tracks with a look of shock on his face. I looked to see what he was looking at. Up ahead at the dock stood my dad. He pointed north along the river.

"Look, Marcie, he's showing us the way," Jim whispered. Then my dad just disappeared.

We both ran to the water and jumped in Jim's boat. I released the dock lines and pushed us off. The engine started on the dime, and we were headed north in the middle of the night.

It was funny how just the start of a boat could make me think of Bill. Bill would be sweet-talking that old motor of his. "What will I do without him?"

"Did you say something, Marcie?" Jim asked.

"No, no … I was just wondering where my dad went." There I was talking to myself again.

I had to hold on to the sides of the boat due to the wind still blowing some and the water whipping up against the boat. We weren't even going fast, but the boat was bucking like a bronco at the rodeo. I was thankful Jim had a searchlight on board. I turned it on while trying to steady myself. I could see a light up ahead.

"Look Jim, there's a light," I yelled.

When we got closer to the light on shore, we noticed my dad. It was as if he was standing on the bank of the river waiting for us. He seemed to glow with a light from within. I had never seen someone look so beautiful. He looked like an angel. The light in and around him radiated so strongly that there was no darkness anywhere near him. The woods took on a magical glow, even though it was pitch black.

Jim slowed the boat and veered toward my dad at the water's edge. As we got closer, my dad turned and started walking away from us into the woods. I turned excitedly to Jim. "Hurry so we don't lose him!"

I threw down the searchlight and jumped from the boat before we even touched the land. With my foot half in the water and half out, I started running toward my dad. I had on my new rubber boots, blue jeans, and a loose-fitting cotton shirt, and my hair was tied back. I ran like the wind into the woods, following the light. I could hear Jim close behind me. It was kind of funny that I was following a light in the woods again. *I wonder if there is some kind of significance to this.*

All of a sudden my dad stopped. I also stopped dead in my tracks, waiting to see what to do next. He pointed toward a huge old oak tree. Its branches, hung thickly with moss, were swaying in the wind.

I looked closer and saw a large, dark opening in this old tree. I walked slowly toward the opening when I saw movement. Something was coming out of the huge hole in the base of the tree. My breath caught in my throat. Fear was gripping me so I couldn't even move. Was it a bear or an alligator?

Jim brushed past me to the tree. He knelt down, and I could tell he was pulling up on something. It was Bill. Jim was pulling Bill to his feet.

I couldn't move. I was in shock. I turned, and my dad was gone. The darkness enveloped us like the murky waters of the bayous.

"Marcie? Marcie?" Jim yelled loudly.

I came out of this daze and still just stood there. I was afraid to move. Afraid of what, I don't know. Maybe I was afraid to see if Bill was hurt or what.

"Marcie, get on the move, girl," Jim yelled. "Help me here!"

I jumped toward Bill and grabbed him. He was damp, cold and shaking. Jim kept asking, "Bill, are you all right?" Bill never uttered a word. All I could think was that he must be in shock. Where was his boat? How did he get here? How did he even find this big oak tree, big enough to shelter a full-grown person from the wind and rain?

We walked back through the woods to the boat. Luckily, it was still there, with the wind and all. Jim hadn't even tied it down.

We positioned Bill in the boat and headed back to the dock. The wind was still blowing, and all I could do was sit next to Bill in the boat and hold him close to me. He was still shivering. It was still so dark, I couldn't even see if he was hurt, and he sure wasn't volunteering any information.

I found myself praying: *Please, Lord, take care of my Bill. Please let my Bill be okay. I need him, Lord. He's a good man. Please let him be all right. Thank you, Dad, for helping me find my man. Thank You, Lord, for letting my dad help. I don't know what I would have done without his help.*

All of a sudden Bill turned to look at me. "Bill? Are you all right?" He bent near and kissed me on my forehead, never saying one word.

We made it to the dock in no time. By some strange coincidence, Frank and T Boy were waiting, as if they knew we were coming.

They had just come from my house, where Mom told them that we had left an hour or so ago to go look for Bill. Frank's dad let them borrow the truck to come look for us. And there they were, just in time. They came running down to help Bill out of the boat. Before we knew it, we were all headed to the hospital. On the way I used Frank's cell phone to call Mom. I knew in turn she would be calling others.

Through streets swollen with water, we finally made it to the hospital, where family and friends were gathering. People in hospital uniforms took Bill and rushed him to the back. After what seemed like hours, the doctor came out and talked to Bill's mom. What was he saying? *Man, I wish I had taken lip reading class.* Bill's mom then turned to tell everyone to go on home; he was fine with just some scrapes and bruises, and they were just keeping him overnight for observation. It was said they had put him in the same room with his dad, who was also being kept overnight.

We all started walking toward the door when Bill's mom grabbed my arm lightly. "You don't have to go, Marcie; I know Bill would want you here."

I smiled at her and said, "Thanks, but I believe I'll go. I'll come check on him in the morning."

"As you wish," she whispered.

I wasn't all that close to Bill's family. They seemed to be good people, and Bill thought the world of them. His mom was short in stature with short brown hair that was graying on the sides. Her name was Sarah, and she was a beautician in town. Bill's dad, whose name was Richard, had worked offshore his whole life. Bill also had an older brother who lived in Houston. He was some kind of businessman and made good money.

It felt good to know that Sarah had asked me to stay, but my insecurities were in high gear right now. *If Bill is okay, then why wasn't he talking? How can this have happened? Why would he go out there in the middle of the night alone? Alone!* I'd never been so worried in all my life, and I didn't like the feeling.

All I could hear in my head were all the words my dad told me growing up, about not giving your heart to anyone. "If you give your heart, Marcie, you will be hurt."

I needed to get out of this hospital. *It's only been a couple of weeks since I was in here, and I just can't trust my judgment right now. Did Jim and I really see my dad again?*

Everyone was waiting for me outside. Frank gave us all a ride home.

"You're awfully quiet, Marcie," Jim said. "What's on your mind?"

"Nothing. It's just been a long and unusual night, and I'm ready to go home and go to bed."

"I know that's right," Jim smiled. He winked at me, "You do know everything will be okay, right?"

"Of course, yes, I-I know," I stuttered.

I still didn't know how Jim knew, but he always seemed to know when I wasn't feeling right.

The weather had finally eased, leaving debris everywhere. The ditches were all swelling with water. Frank pulled up at the house and dropped me off. I waved my good-byes and ran inside. The house was dark and quiet, and I knew Mom was in bed, which was where I was headed. I just didn't want to think anymore. I wanted my mind to shut up. I wanted to let this day go, lie down on my bed, and get some sleep.

It wasn't long before I fell asleep. Again my dream brought me to a beautiful place, a place beyond description. Everything was so crisp and fresh that it was as though every sense in my body was alive. I could smell what seemed like a fresh rain. My body felt at peace and full of love. It was a place where I felt every emotion, every desire in my very being. I didn't seem to have a care in the world. This must be the peace of God, and it was overpowering. Just like my previous dream, the colors jumped out at me as if I had never seen true colors before, as if my life on earth was dull in comparison to this place.

I glanced at the trees and the lake before me. One willow tree seemed to beckon me to go sit under it. Who was I, not to go sit in this beautiful place and relax and enjoy this wonderful dream? I was looking out at the lake when I knew I was not alone. There was no fear, just a curiosity about who could be there. I looked around but saw no one.

As I continued to just sit and enjoy the utter serenity I noticed that someone was appearing before me. Was it my dad? No, it wasn't. This man stood before me in robes. He looked to be in his thirties. He had a kind face, and he seemed to glow from within, just the way my dad did. All I could do was stare at him.

"Marcie, I have had my eye on you," said the stranger.

"Do I know you?" I asked.

"You do, but you don't," he said.

"Excuse me?" I whispered.

"You hear my voice all the time, but you don't know it's me."

"Oh, okay." I replied as I rolled my eyes.

"I know what you're thinking, Marcie."

"Oh really?" I asked, a little flippantly.

"You're thinking this is only a dream, so just go with it."

"How did you know?" I asked in astonishment.

"Because Marcie girl, I know everything about you. We are one."

"We are one what?" I asked.

"We are all connected," the stranger said with a smile.

"I still don't know who you are, sir."

"I am your best friend, Marcie. I have been with you since birth. My name is Michael. I am your spirit guide, or some may call me an angel."

"Okay," I said, standing up. "You're an angel, and I'm the tooth fairy." I huffed. "Listen, sir, I'm going home. I've had about enough close encounters. It's totally over my head, and I just don't want to know or think about all this hocus-pocus anymore."

"Marcie, you can't escape truth regardless how hard you try," the man said.

"You know, I used to lead a normal life, and all of a sudden one day it all changed. Now nothing makes sense anymore. I feel like I'm in the Twilight Zone or something." I said, exasperated.

"Marcie, I assure you, you are not in the Twilight Zone. This is real." The man went on, "You grieved so much over your dad that we decided to help you understand what is going on."

"But all this stuff is so weird, and I really don't want to discuss it with you, a stranger."

"I understand your frustration about this side of your life. It's like going through life without your twin sibling, and then out of the blue one day someone comes up to you and says, 'Hey, I'm your twin, and I want to be in your life.' All those years you went through life never knowing you even had a twin.

"It's hard to know you have a spiritual side too, because no one has told you, at least not until now. You've been given a special gift," Michael explained, "a gift to know where you are from and why you are here, and a gift to see your dad again."

I hung my head, and tears started welling up in my eyes. "He saved Bill's life."

"As I said, Marcie, you have been given a wonderful gift. People are slowly starting to understand these things. The veil has thinned to the point that more and more people will start to see the truth. You have even been sent a teacher."

"Jim?" I asked.

Michael nodded. "This teacher—Jim, you call him—had such a deep desire within him for spiritual truth that we allowed him to know this truth. You must earn each step you take in life."

"So, Michael, why have you shown yourself to me in this dream, and where is my dad?"

"Your dad is resting. Not in a physical way but in a spiritual way. I am here to tell you that no matter how hard life gets, you are not alone. It may seem you are, but you are not. Life is not always going to be a piece of cake. You will have good times and bad time. But listen to that still, small voice. If the voice is encouraging and loving, listen to what it says because there is also another voice that wants to be heard."

"What voice is that?" I asked.

"There is also a voice in your head that is very strong, but it's not encouraging or loving. It is a deceiver. It condemns you and tells you that you can't do anything right. Listening to that voice can hurt your soul and keep you from moving forward. Stand firm, Marcie." Michael was slowing disappearing before my eyes.

*Beep, beep, beep.* My hand reached over and turned off the alarm clock. "Oh man, what the hell?" I said, half asleep. I felt as if I had cotton in my mouth. *What kind of dream was that? I can't seem to get away from any of this spooky stuff, even in my dreams.*

I rolled over and sat up on the side of the bed. *I just don't know what to think anymore. My mind is so tired of all this. But I can't deny the things I've seen and heard. Unless I have totally lost my mind, and I need a straitjacket.*

I stepped into my slippers, grabbed my robe, and walked to the kitchen. I could already smell the fresh brewed coffee. *Now, this is real. Coffee is real. Now, coffee I believe in.* I giggled at myself.

Mom came around the corner in the kitchen. "Oh, Marcie girl, you're up early. You want some breakfast?"

"Yes ma'am," I said sleepily.

"You going to the hospital to bring Bill home?" Mom asked.

I hung my head and mumbled, "No, I don't think so."

"What are you saying, girl? Speak up."

I looked her in the eyes and said, "No, I'm just going out to the pasture and check on everything."

Her smile faded away. "You know, Marcie if you love Bill, you need to stand by him at this time. Do you love him, Marcie?"

I hesitated. "Yes, I guess."

"Girl, what are you thinking? You know darn well you love Bill. So why are you dragging your feet now?"

"I don't know, Mom." I pulled my legs onto the chair and hugged my ankles. I laid my head on my knees.

"You are obviously concerned about something. So what is it?"

Tears started running down my cheek. "Mom," my voice squeaked, "I put my heart out there. I almost lost him in that terrible storm. I've never known such fear. When I thought I'd lost him, my heart ached. I mean it really ached. I just don't want to feel that way again."

"So you're going to run away from him so you won't feel anymore. How selfish of you. You're thinking of running away from love and letting Bill down at the same time. Marcie, he is your best friend. You can't just run away from him. He loves you, and you love him. Little girl, I have never known you to run away from any situation or to be as confused about anything as you have been when it concerns Bill." Then she smiled.

I looked at her with a questioning look. "What, Mom? Why are you smiling?"

"You really love him. Nothing has ever blindsided you like loving Bill." She laughed as she got up and started walking away from the kitchen.

I had to admit she was right. I had always been strong, and never had I run from a fight. *But this has totally scared the pants off me. Who would ever have thought "Love" could knock me off my feet like this?* I had to laugh too, listening to my mom still laughing in her bedroom. Then she started to sing.

*"Marcie and Bill sitting in the tree, K-I-S-S-I-N-G."*

How funny. All of a sudden my heart felt light. "What am I doing? I do love Bill. I never have to lose him again. I can give him my whole heart and soul and never lose him. How stupid I have been. I should run over there and jump into his arms. Again, I'm talking to myself like an idiot." I jumped to my feet and ran to put my clothes on. *Yep, I'm going to be by his side.*

In a matter of minutes I was running out the door. "Bye, Mom. I'm going to the hospital," I yelled as I slammed the door.

Less than a half-hour later I walked into the hospital, on cloud nine. I couldn't wait to see Bill.

Sarah, Bill's mom, was sitting in the waiting room. I walked up and asked, "How is Bill?"

"Oh, dear, I didn't see you come in. Bill and his dad are fine. They are getting dressed as we speak." She stood up and put her hands on my shoulders. "Dear, Bill has been through a really rough time, and he is tired. He doesn't want to see anyone right now."

My heart sank. "What?"

"Bill just wants to go home. He told me he doesn't want to see anyone."

"But I'm Marcie," I said.

"I know, dear. I think he just needs some time alone for now. You understand, don't you?"

"Yes ma'am. Just tell him I came, okay?"

"Yes, yes dear, of course," she said with a smile.

I walked out of the hospital, dragging my heart behind me. *What has happened? Sarah couldn't wait for me to stay last night, and now Bill doesn't want to see me. Didn't he kiss me on my forehead only last night? I just don't understand. Here I am ready to give my life to this man, and he turns me aside like an old worn-out shoe.* I could feel a stabbing in my heart. It was as if my world was gone. I walked back to my little car, not even seeing the beauty of the sun shining and the flowers in bloom after that terrible storm.

"How could this day have turned out like this? I'm not going to worry. He'll be calling. He loves me. Everything will be okay. It has to. It just has to. He'll come to his senses. After all, he can't go fishing without me, can he?

"Again, I am talking out loud to myself. I really need to check into this. I don't think people talk out loud to themselves like this. This should be an internal conversation and not for the world to hear."

With tears streaming down my cheeks, I made my way home slowly and in complete bewilderment, my heart aching so much it was almost unbearable.

# CHAPTER 11

The next couple of days were uneventful, just regular days full of chores. Mom couldn't believe that Bill wouldn't call or see me. She said I must have done something to this wonderful man to keep him from calling me. I quit calling him after getting my fifth excuse from his mom and decided to just give him space.

"Hey, girl. What you up to?" I heard from behind me. It was Jim. I turned and ran into his arms.

"Hey, hey, what's all this about?" Jim held me for a while; then he put me at arm's length, looked me in the eye, and said, "Something doesn't feel right. What's going on?"

"How do you do that, Jim?" I asked.

"What?"

"How do you always know when something is wrong in my life? Are you psychic or something?"

"It's called being sensitive to others," Jim said softly. "So, my little girl, tell me: what's going on?"

All I could do was look at him. I was afraid that if I spoke and told him what was happening, I would just start crying all over again.

After a minute he asked, "It's Bill, isn't it?"

"Yes," I said. Tears were starting to well up in my eyes again.

"He's okay, isn't he?"

"Yes, yes. It's not that. He doesn't want to talk to me."

"What? I thought you two were an item." Concern was evident on his face.

"Well, we're not," I snapped back as I started to walk away.

"Did he tell you why?" Jim followed me, trying to keep up.

"No, that's what's funny." I stopped and looked at Jim holding my tears back. "He didn't even have the decency to tell me why he doesn't want to talk to me anymore."

"He'll come around. You'll see," Jim said with a wink.

"Yeah, that's kind of what I told myself too."

"That wasn't you, girly. That was your spirit guide."

"Oh no, here we go again. I don't want to talk hocus-pocus right now."

"It's not." Jim smiled. "It's real. When you hear encouraging words in your mind, it's your angel or spirit guide reassuring you. They are very encouraging. They love you very much and are on your side."

"Yeah," I growled, "so I've been told."

"What? Are you holding out on me, Marcie?" Jim asked.

"Well, I kind of had another dream the other night. This man came to me claiming to be my spirit guide, and he told me he has always been with me."

"Ahaa," Jim responded. "When they come in dreams, it's because we won't recognize them in our minds or in our hearts, but they do make themselves known sometimes. What else did he say?"

"He told me his name was Michael, and he told me about listening to the right voice, just like you told me."

"Great Marcie, that is confirmation. So how many spirit guides did you see in the dream?" Jim asked.

"Only the one."

"Did the spirit guide have wings? What did he look like?"

"He looked like a man in his thirties. He was wearing some robes, and no, he did not have wings."

"And where were you in the dream?"

"I was sitting under a beautiful willow tree looking out on a wonderful lake. The colors were out of this world." I could tell by the look on Jim's face and the way he leaned in to catch every word that he was really interested in my dream.

"You know, Marcie, it still excites me when I hear things like this. I believe they came to you in a place that you are used to or comfortable with, like your favorite tree, so you wouldn't be scared. You know how you love that old willow tree that you're always sitting under?"

"Yeah, that's where I think and relax."

"Yep, they knew that being someplace familiar would calm you so you wouldn't be afraid. You weren't afraid, were you?"

"No. Actually, I was kind of mad that I was put in that weird situation again," I explained.

"Are you still having problems with all the things I've been trying to teach you?"

"Like I told Michael, 'spirit guide'"—I made quotation marks in the air with my fingers—"you have to realize I was leading a perfectly normal life until my first contact with my dad. I was in control and knew what I wanted. Now I feel like my world has been turned upside down, and I don't know which end is up. It's like an emotional roller coaster. I don't know what to do with my life anymore. I have this terrible battle going on in my head. One minute I know what I want, and I'm listening to you and my dad, and the next I'm back to where I was before."

Jim intervened. "Marcie, the only reason this is happening to you is that you are straddling the fence. You are struggling; it's between what you have always done and this new way of life. Change does not come easy. Once you have accepted this completely, you won't have that feeling of your world being upside down. Trust that voice within."

"Oh Jim, another thing that's been happening to me is that I talk to myself all the time now."

"Do you feel, my little girl, that you are carrying on a conversation or just mulling things over out loud?" he asked.

"Well, I think both. Do you have an explanation for that, too?" I said with a smirk on my face.

"If you find yourself carrying on a conversation with yourself, you are probably talking to your spirit guide or angel. But if you find yourself mulling things over and over in your head, then you're probably just going over things from the day with yourself.

"What else do you want to know?" Jim asked with a smile on his face.

I put my head down and mumbled. "Do you think Bill hates me?"

"Marcie, listen to me, you know better than that. Bill loves you."

"Then what the hell is his problem, Jim?"

We both were interrupted by a movement in the trees. It was T Boy. He wore his old faded overalls and his new alligator boots and had a big smile on his face. I was so happy to see him that I couldn't keep from running into his arms. He picked me up and swung me around. Then he put me down. "Mais, Cher, it's good to lay eyes on you too."

"It's so good to see you, T Boy. I feel like I've lost all my friends, and things will never be the same again."

"Dat not true, Cher. In fact, I was coming here to remind you of our yearly crawfish boil."

"Oh yeah, the annual crawfish boil. Will Bill be coming?" I asked with my head tilted to see him against the blinding sun.

"I'm headed dat way now."

"So we having our crawfish boil by the river, as always?" I asked.

T Boy nodded. "Me and Frank, we get them little rascals Friday afternoon, so we be ready for Saturday."

"I'll be in charge of the taters, onions, corn, and crawfish boil," I said.

"Hay dar, Swamp Man, you come too?" T Boy hadn't talked this much all year.

Jim asked, "Is there anything I can bring?"

"How about a full ice chest?" I smiled, and T Boy smiled.

"You in charge of the ice, Swamp Man." T Boy said excited.

Jim smiled at his new nickname and at being included in a gathering.

My heart was busting open, to know that all the gang would be together. *Maybe things can get back to normal again*, I wished silently.

T Boy was headed down the road. He never let grass grow under his feet. Nine times out of ten, he walked everywhere he went. He always said, "Mais, I got to get my exercise somehow." *Well, at least he has good boots now,* I thought.

I turned to Jim. "I sure hope Bill comes."

"Why wouldn't he, girl?"

"I just don't know. Something is wrong. Maybe I said something wrong. Maybe I didn't do something that I should have. Maybe he's mad because I didn't stay at the hospital with him. Maybe—"

"Whoa there, Marcie, stop it right now. Come, let's go sit on the porch. I have another lesson for you." He smiled. "Actually, it's the same lesson but put in a way you may understand better."

I sat in my dad's rocker on the porch, and Jim pulled a chair across from me and looked me straight in the face. In fact, his stare kind of unnerved me. Then he gently leaned over and touched my hand.

"Listen, Marcie, it's taken me a long time to learn this lesson, and I'm still working on it, but here goes.

"From the moment we wake up we are deciding what to do. Do I turn off the alarm clock or hit snooze? Do I wear the black pants and the blue shirt or the blue pants and the black shirt? Should I tell my friend the truth or only part of it? Our mind is always talking to us. Remember when your spirit guide told you to listen to the right voice?"

"Yeah, I remember."

Jim continued, "We also judge situations. Your mind is telling you, you must have done something wrong. You know, our mind beats us up all the time. We are stupid, retarded, lazy, and selfish. On and on our mind condemns us. According to us, we are the worst person alive, and God will never forgive us. We feel inadequate to control our own lives. What's really bad is we condemn others without even knowing the full story.

"Many years ago I was a church hopper. I would find a church I liked, and then I would condemn other churches because I felt they weren't right. I felt the Baptist church I was in at the time was right. Then I'd change religions, and then I felt the Baptist church was wrong and the Catholic church was right. Then I'd change religions again and felt the Pentecostal was right and everyone else was wrong. Then in the end, when I quit going to church altogether, I felt all religions were wrong, and I was right for not going to church.

"Well, I really had a good talking to with myself on this. First, why was I judging all these religions? Second, who was right and who was wrong? I judged everything according to what I was taught and what I thought to be right. No matter what religion or church I decided to study, I found lots of right and lots of wrong with them. I was judging again and again. So after several years of not going to church and just reading my Bible, I realized no one is right and no one is wrong. I was missing the whole message of God.

"I had gotten so self-righteous that I would even pray and ask God to change these people for what they were doing. I should have asked God to change my heart and mind, not theirs. I was practicing witchcraft for praying prayers that I thought was right for that person, not realizing that maybe they needed to be on this journey in that church or needed to go through these hard times to grow stronger. Who was I to know what's best for someone else, according to the crap I was taught in church or school or by my parents or worst of all by my ego? So I learned to trust God to take care of everyone. Now when I pray for someone, I pray for God's best in their life to happen. Who knows best but God?

"So all this judging you're doing in your mind about Bill will make you crazy. Remember judging Bill and Mary Ann at the party? Remember judging if Bill would be okay or not when he was in that storm? It's no different. Don't judge yourself. There is no judgment in love. Love is accepting. Love is peace of mind. Marcie, take the good with the bad, and just live your life the best you can. Don't judge right or wrong. Just trust God in all things."

"I know you're right, Jim; I feel it in my heart. Everything will be all right. I'll trust God to do what is best for me. Whether Bill comes back to me or not, I'll trust God through all this." I couldn't believe I'd just said that. *I knew it, I knew it—I've turned into a girl. I just as soon put on a dress by the way I'm thinking.*

"Forgive me for repeating myself on some of my lessons to you, but I just want you to be completely comfortable using and learning these techniques."

"That's okay. I guess I need the practice." I smiled. "Jim, can I get you some coffee or something?"

"Sure, kiddo, that would be nice," Jim replied with a smile.

I walked into the kitchen and found my mom crying. "Oh no, Mom, what's wrong?"

She got up from the table and walked over to hug me. "I'm so sorry, Marcie."

"Mom, you're scaring me. What's wrong?"

"It's me, Marcie—I'm wrong."

"Excuse me? What are you talking about?"

"I didn't mean to eavesdrop on yours and Jim's conversation again. I'm sorry. I wanted to say I'm sorry for not believing you when you said it wasn't your fault that Bill wouldn't talk to you. Jim was absolutely right in what he said. I didn't mean to judge you. Your dad would have said what was on his mind to Bill, and you're so much like your dad that I just thought you pushed him away. The best thing in your life and you pushed him away. Please forgive me for my terrible thoughts."

"Of course, Mom." I hugged her close. Then I gave her a wink, "It looks like we are both learning from Jim."

I heard a noise behind me. I looked, and Jim was standing there.

"I was coming to help with the coffee," Jim said softly with a look of embarrassment on his face.

"I guess you heard all that, Jim?"

"Yeah, but I won't hold it against you." We all started laughing.

We got our coffee and sat down at the table. Jim was starting to mean so much to me. It was always so good to be with him. He could turn water into wine all the time, always seeing the best in all situations.

After some chitchat and coffee, Jim said he needed to go, but wanted me to walk him out. *Guess I have another talk coming*, I thought. We walked out and down the steps. He looked back toward the house and then looked at me. I turned to look at the house myself to see what he was looking at. He cleared his throat. I wanted to laugh. He seemed nervous about something.

"I'd like to ask you something, Marcie."

"Okay, what?"

"I'd like your permission to ask your mom out."

"That's what you're nervous about?" I couldn't help it. I started laughing.

"Well? Can I?" he asked.

I was still laughing. I snorted and then laughed even more.

"Marcie, I'm serious here. I want to take your mom out."

"I accept," I heard from behind me. My laughing ended abruptly. I swung around and saw my mom standing at the door. Then I looked back and forth from her to Jim.

"Well, I—I guess since Mom has already accepted your invitation, it would be all right for her to go out with you," I said with a smile.

Jim asked Mom, "How about a crawfish boil Saturday?" He was slowly walking up to her.

"That would be great," she said slowly, turning four shades of red. Jim reached for her hand and raised it to his lips for a light kiss.

Then he raised his head and said, "I'll come by Saturday and walk you over, okay?" Mom nodded.

Jim looked at me with a smile. I couldn't help but smile too. "See you there also." He gave me a wink as he walked away.

I was totally dumbfounded. I couldn't say a word but could only look at Mom. She had a smile and a look on her face that I couldn't say I'd ever seen before.

I walked toward the barn. What was all that about? Since when did Jim find my mom—ah, attractive? *Oh, my God, Mom attractive. But she's my mom. She's a woman too, you know. But she's my Mom. She can't want another man but my dad. But of course she can. Well, it's not like she's marrying the man. But what would I do if she did? Jim as my dad?* "What am I worried about? Jim is a great man. I'd be lucky to have him as my new dad. Wonder where they will live if they get married—in the woods?" I started laughing. *I'm talking to myself again, and I've already got my mom married and living in the woods with the Swamp Man.* I couldn't stop laughing. *Oh, my God, I can't catch my breath; this is just too funny.*

# CHAPTER 12

The morning sun was streaming through the flowered curtains of my room as I rolled over and sat up, hanging my legs over the side of the bed. *I know I'm supposed to be excited about today and seeing Bill, but I'm scared shitless. I can only imagine what Bill is going to tell me. Or maybe he won't even show up. No, he'll show up, and we'll talk this over.* "We'll either go on being friends, or we'll go our separate ways. Everything will be okay; you worry too much." *Well, here we go again. Am I talking to myself, or am I talking to my new friend on the other side, like Jim said? If it's true I'm just carrying on a conversation with Michael, then,* "Thanks for the pep talk, Michael."

*I can actually see what Jim was saying. I'm totally negative.* "Have I always been negative and judgmental like this?" |

"Of course you have; you're human."

"Oh, my God, it's true. —Is this Michael?" I asked.

"Yes. I'm always with you, Marcie."

"So can you tell me if Bill is coming today?"

"Yes, he is."

"Will we talk?"

"Yes, you will. You will come to an understanding."

"Understanding about what?"

"I'm not your personal fortune teller, Marcie."

I giggled. "Okay, okay. I get it. I have a lot to do today anyway, so I'll talk to you later."

I was in the kitchen pouring coffee when Mom walked in. "So Mom, since when did you start thinking of Jim as"—I paused—"you know, as a man?"

Mom giggled. "Of course he's a man."

"You know what I mean, Mom."

"What are you worried about, Marcie? I thought you liked Jim."

"I do."

"Well, look at it this way. First, I'm not getting married, just going down to the bayou for some crawfish. Second, could you actually see me with any other man in this area of Louisiana?" Her smile faded. "Or maybe you can't see me with any man but your dad."

"You know, Dad's the only man I've ever seen you with. It's been you and Dad my whole life. It's just hard to see you with anyone but Dad, I guess." I walked out of the room at that comment.

Today had come before I felt ready in my heart. I couldn't help but fear that things would not come out right. How I wished I could control my negative thoughts. Even though I heard encouraging words from my spirit guide all the time, it was like a battle was going on in my mind. But Jim was right: the positive did always seem to outweigh the negative.

Mom was humming a song and getting ready, and I was about done getting all the goodies ready for the crawfish boil. My day's chores would be on hold until this afternoon when we finished with the crawfish boil. I loaded up the back of the small flatbed trailer with everything I could think of for the boil. Soon all that remained to get were some folding chairs.

I could see Jim walking up from the dirt road on this beautiful Saturday.

"We couldn't have picked a better day for a crawfish boil."

"That's just what I was thinking," I said with a smile. I was lugging some folding chairs to the flatbed.

"Can I help you with that, Marcie?" he asked.

"Sure, grab a couple more chairs in the shed."

"Say, are you all right about me taking your mom to the crawfish boil?" Jim asked, sounding a bit nervous.

"No problem, Jim."

"Well, are you worried about Bill?"

"I think you know the answer to that one."

"I do know, but I was wondering how you were handling it. Do you need a pep talk or anything?"

"Jim, I recognized Michael in my thoughts this morning. We talked, and I know that Bill and I will come to an understanding. Not sure what kind of understanding. But at least that sounds good."

Jim smiled and said, "That does sound good."

"Well, I'll see you and Mom later. I'm headed to our crawfish spot. See y'all in a little bit, unless y'all need a ride on the flatbed."

"No, I think we'll walk. It's too pretty of a day, and your mom and I can talk some," Jim said.

"Okay, then, see you later." I waved as I hopped in the truck.

When I got to the water, only T Boy was there. He was setting up the outdoor gas burner with a huge pot of water on top. Crawfish were already purging in salt water.

It wasn't long before Frank showed with his portion of the feast. As I set up some folding tables and chairs, Mom and Jim walked up. They seemed to be in deep conversation. Mom's laughter floated to my ears. I couldn't help but smile, knowing she was having a good time already.

It was a beautiful day. The bayou was calm, with just the slightest ripples from a slow moving breeze and only an occasional fish jumping. The midmorning sun was shining on the water, and maybe a half dozen turtles were sunbathing on the fallen logs in the water. A couple of white egrets on the opposite bank, with the backdrop of trees, made a beautiful picture. I let out a sigh.

T Boy interrupted my thoughts. "Mais, what be taking Bill so long to get here?"

I wondered if he would even show up. But lo and behold, just then Bill was pulling his truck under a big black oak tree. He was overloaded with several six-packs of beer and another of Coke. He really looked good. I hadn't realized how much I missed him till I saw him.

Bill passed right by me without a word and went straight to the table near T Boy to unload the beers into the ice chest that Jim had left earlier in the day.

I couldn't believe he hadn't even acknowledged me. My heart seemed to drop like a stone. He turned and started talking to T Boy and Frank. *He's just going to ignore me. I'll show him.* I stomped right past the table, grabbed my keys, and started to leave.

Jim ran up to me. "Where are you going?"

"He didn't even say hi to me. He just passed right by me."

"Okay, okay, Marcie. Remember what I told you. Do everything in love."

"Oh my God, here we go again. What love? If he loved me at all even in the least, at least he would act like it!" My heart was starting to hurt again.

"Don't run away, Marcie. Don't let his actions push your buttons. Tell him hi, and just continue doing what you're doing."

"You're right; I shouldn't run away," I said as I straightened my shoulders. "But what if he doesn't respond?"

"It's not about what he says or does; it's how you handle the situation. So if he doesn't respond, just keep on cooking or cleaning or whatever you're doing. As long as you do everything in love, even if it looks like it's not working, give it time. Love has a way of working on people, even the hardest of hearts."

I straightened my shirt, pushed my hair up, and shook it into long waves down my back. Then I walked toward Bill. I felt like I was going to be sick. My nerves were starting to take effect. I was ready to turn and run with my tail between my legs. But I kept myself together.

"Hi, Bill. It's good to see you're doing well." I managed to say it all without losing my composure.

He turned and looked at me. "It's—it's good to be doing well." He then turned and started talking to Frank again.

I grabbed a bottle of beer, twisted the top off, took a swig, and started getting some trays ready for the crawfish. I then made my famous secret sauce. I walked back to the guys and started carrying on a conversation with Frank and T Boy.

"So where did you get the crawfish, guys?"

"We found some in Simmesport," Frank responded. "A guy there has been crawfishing for ten years. He had a really good price too."

"That's great," I said.

I heard T Boy clear his throat. I looked at him, and he nodded toward Jim and Mom. "Mais, we got us a couple over dar." We all turned and looked at Jim and Mom.

I smiled. "It sure looks like it," I murmured.

"Dat be real nice," T Boy said with a smile.

I walked back to the far side of the flatbed trailer to make sure I had everything and to stay busy. Finding nothing, I turned to leave and walked right into Bill.

"Oh, I'm sorry," I said. I started to walk past him, but he stepped right in front of me.

"Marcie, I guess it's as good a time as any to talk to you." I stopped short and looked him in the eyes to try and read what he was thinking.

"Something weird happened to me that night of the storm." I backed up so I could lean on the truck. He continued, "It was dark that night, and the wind was terrible. I had already made a round to the left of the river then headed to the right."

I knew exactly what he was talking about. The river he was commenting on is shaped similar to a sideward horse shoe. You could go left of the dock or right of the dock.

"The boat was rocking so bad, I started to give it a little more throttle hoping to keep it from bouncing so much. I didn't even see the log sticking up in the water, but the boat hit it, and I went flying. When I came up from the water, I saw something."

"What?" I asked.

"You're not going to believe me. I'm still not sure I saw what I think I saw."

"Well, what did you see?" I demanded.

"I have gone over and over in my head how to tell you this, and there is no easy way. So I'm just going to just say it. I—I saw something bright. When my eyes focused better I saw, I saw …."

"What, Bill, what did you see?" I asked.

"I saw your dad." he blurted out.

I laughed. "That's what all this is about?"

"This is not funny, Marcie. Your dad is dead."

I laughed even harder.

"You don't believe me." Bill said exasperated.

I calmed down a little. "I do believe you."

"No, you don't. You're laughing at me."

"No, I'm not laughing at you. So is this why you have been avoiding me?"

"Marcie, I don't believe in ghosts. I know this sounds like total nonsense. But your dad showed me where to go to get out of the weather."

"Bill, how did you think we found you?" I said with a relieved smile.

"Excuse me?"

"We followed my dad," I haltingly explained. "He showed us where to find you. We might never have found you; we could have been out there for hours. We didn't see your boat."

"My boat? Shit, that boat is long gone." He sighed." I guess it's under the water."

"He came to help us find you, Bill."

"Marcie, stop!" Bill yelled.

I jerked my head and looked at him.

"Marcie, you know me. I'm a meat and potato guy. I fish, I fix cars. I'm a simple man, Marcie. I don't go for this sort of thing. This kind of stuff is hard to believe. And if I hadn't seen it myself, I would never have believed it."

"But, Bill, you did see him."

"I wondered if I really did. It's been hard for me to accept," he said with a sad look on his face.

"Is this why you have pushed me away?" I asked.

"I know I've been acting funny, and avoiding you. It's because—well, I didn't think you'd believe me. Also, I don't want to think of this. I want to put it behind me and move on."

I hung my head and felt the tears starting to run down my face. "I didn't mean to upset you, Marcie. You have to realize I haven't been able to tell anyone about this. You're the first. I couldn't avoid telling you that I saw your dad. Please, don't cry." He reached over and brushed the tears from my face.

"Bill, I have to tell you something too."

"Oh shit, what?" Bill asked.

"That's not the first time I've seen my dad. I've seen him several times."

"What?"

"First time was the night we went to your camp for a frog leg dinner. I saw him on the road. Then I've dreamed of him several times."

"Whoa, stop. I don't want to hear all this."

"Please, Bill. Who can I talk to about all this, if not with my best friend?"

"I'm sorry, but I can't do this." He turned and started to walk away.

I yelled at him. "What, you've got to be kidding me. You're walking away from me again. So what? You're going to ignore me again and push me away."

He stopped in his tracks. He turned and looked at me. My heart was on the fence. I caught my breath.

"Bye, Marcie," he said as he walked away.

I couldn't believe what had just happened. Where was the "come to an understanding" that Michael talked about?

"Bill," I yelled. I paused. "Still friends?"

Again, he stopped in his tracks. He turned and walked back to me. He gripped my shoulders. "Marcie, we have been friends a long time. I love you more than my left arm. But like I said, I don't ever want to talk about this. I'll walk away from you in a heartbeat if you ever mention any of this again. Do you understand me?"

For the first time I understood what Jim meant when he said his choice for more knowledge of spiritual things outweighed his family. His wife didn't want anything to do with all this stuff, so he left. He felt knowledge was more important to him.

"Bill, I love you too, but I feel you're asking me to choose between you and my dad."

"Marcie, your dad is dead. I'm not."

"But I feel there is so much to learn from my dad."

"Marcie, as much as I don't want to, I'm walking away from you. I feel you have made your choice." Again, he turned and walked away.

I didn't stop him. I stood there dumbfounded. Jim came from around the truck.

"I didn't mean to eavesdrop, but I heard everything."

I still just stood there in disbelief. I felt as if a knife was stabbing me in my chest. It felt so real that I had to put a hand there to see where the pain was coming from.

Jim put an arm around my shoulder and guided me to a chair to sit down. I could feel every eye on me. I looked up, and sure enough T Boy, Frank, and Mom stood there looking at me. Had they heard the whole conversation? I hung my head.

Jim was slowly and politely reassuring me. "I can go talk to him if you want."

"No, no, I just don't know what to make of it all." My heart ached so much, I wanted to cry. But when I looked up everyone was surrounding me.

Frank asked, "Where did Bill go? Is he coming back?"

"No, I don't think so." I couldn't help myself; tears started streaming down my face.

T Boy walked up and grabbed my hand. "Aw, Cher, please don't cry. Bill, he know he got himself a good woman. He'll be back, Cher. But shee, if he don't, I'll take you for myself." I looked up, and T Boy winked at me. I dried my tears. "Now, Cher, give me a smile." I couldn't help myself; I smiled up at T Boy for such a wonderful gesture. "That be my girl."

"Now let's eat some crawfish," Frank said with excitement in his voice. We all headed toward the table.

T Boy was pouring crawfish all over the table. Frank was getting beers for everyone. Mom was making sure we all had some hand towels; napkins didn't work with this bunch. A hand towel was all you could use with these messy, hot crawfish. My secret sauce was already fixed and handed out.

Then we all sat and ate and ate and ate. There was no talking. We all were peeling and dipping and eating. T Boy and Frank were sucking heads and getting every bit of juice possible. Even though it was normal for us to be busy eating and not talking, it just seemed that a dark blanket had dropped over us. I could feel a kind of sadness had settled over the gang; without Bill, it just wasn't complete.

# CHAPTER 13

It had been several months since the crawfish boil. Rumor had it that Bill had packed some bags and left town that same day. No one knew where he went, or they just weren't saying.

T Boy had been coming around more to check on me and Mom. Even Frank made more of an effort to visit. No one had mentioned anything about the day Bill left. It was just regular everyday work on the farm for me. Nothing new, and nothing even seemed out of the ordinary—except my heart. My heart felt so empty. The only man that held my heart in his hands, that I considered my best friend, had just dropped off the face of the earth—and all because he saw my dad. *What's up with that?*

Of course Jim was over a lot. When I say a lot, I mean a lot. We had many talks, and as always he was supportive and generous. He always talked to me in love. I really think I would not have made it without his encouraging talks.

In one of our talks, while I was crying uncontrollably, he mentioned that maybe I needed to change my life in some way.

His quote was "If you always do what you've always done, you'll always get what you've always gotten." After thinking over this saying for a week, I finally decided to get a part-time job in town. It kept me busy and definitely kept my mind off Bill. I was a waitress at a family restaurant called Nanny's. I kept up with my chores at home and then went to work. I was even considering going back to school like Frank.

The spirit world had also been somewhat quiet, even though my mind was never at rest. I came to understand the difference between my own thoughts and the thoughts of my spirit guide.

Fighting against my own thoughts of negativity was an every-second challenge. I did my best to replace my negative thoughts with positive ones. I used positive speeches to myself all the time. Doing this daily helped put me in a better frame of mind. I also noticed, with confrontations at work, that sometimes I could change negative circumstances with positive reinforcement to make better choices in my actions and speak positive affirmation to cover negative thoughts. I was still a work in progress.

Thanks to the long talks with Jim, I also came to learn that this temporary world had many heartaches and difficulties, but once you cross over to the other side, that's not even a part of you anymore. It's not all the difficulties of this world that you think about on the other side but the love you left behind. You leave the opportunity to make a difference in someone else's life—which makes a difference in yours. So even though I didn't need to work, I found that in serving others, even by being a waitress, I was giving of myself.

Mom and I also made homemade praline candy, the way my grandmother made it to give to people going through hard times. So it seemed I was continuously learning and growing through all the adversity in my life. I realized that if I didn't have hard times,

I would never learn how to overcome them. My life had been so predictable, and I was just Marcie, one of the guys. Now I found that I was changing and coming into a new me.

As hard as it was to give of myself, especially when my very heart had been dropped and broken into a thousand tiny pieces, it still helped. It filled another part of my heart with joy, the pure joy of giving. I noticed that even giving a smile to a grumpy old man at the checkout counter at the grocery store lifted my spirits. I never knew how hard it was to fight for the positive. This old man was complaining and harassing the cashier and everyone in line with his negative remarks. He was so negative that he almost tripped over his bottom lip just because the cashier was new and the line was long and moving slowly.

I wanted to join in on his negative pity party, but I took Jim's advice and tried turning the situation around. I smiled. The old man looked at me like I had two heads. I found myself complimenting him on his patience and understanding, when honestly, that was not his strong point. By calling something that was not as if it were, then, lo and behold the man changed right before my eyes. Once his mood changed, everyone around him started to change. It was like a heavy darkness had just dissipated.

It's funny how much a person can grow with the right positive influences. Jim was a true jewel. Sure, a lot of his sayings were difficult to understand, but he never once judged me. He would turn a circumstance around to see not only one side of the coin but both sides. He interpreted the Bible in ways I had never heard it before. He said that, to take the Bible in black and white, you'd swear we were all headed to hell in a handbasket. The way Jim interpreted the Word of God was like listening to birds singing praise—positive, uplifting, and never judging me for not meeting certain standards. I might not have felt loved by some around me, but in God's eyes I was one of His, and He loved me for me. He loved me "just as I am." Jim explained that God was not just a God of the world outside but a God of everything and everywhere. That seemed to give me a lot of comfort.

Jim explained that God spoke to us not only in Scripture but in the sky, in the wind, in nature. He said if we would listen, He was speaking to us all the time.

I also noticed a change in Jim too. The voodoo man of the swamps was coming out of his shell. He no longer hid out deep in the swamps of Louisiana. He was making more and more contacts in town. He was slowly introducing this love idea to people in a way that was not offensive. Best of all, they were listening.

Jim was becoming a great teacher—though of course, some people would never accept this teaching of his. He and mom also had hit it off very well. It seemed that everyone Jim touched grew to be a better person. Mom was singing and humming and smiling like I had never seen before. I knew she still missed Dad, but her whole outlook on life had made a dramatic change for the better.

*If only Bill could be here sitting with me under my favorite tree, soaking in the Louisiana heat and learning the many lessons of Jim. Where could he be? What is he doing? Most of all, why did he run away? I pray he is not one of those people who can't change and see things in a different light. I just can't imagine what my life would be like without Bill.*

Tears started to well up in my eyes. *Daddy, how I wish you were here.* Out of nowhere it was like the world became completely quiet. Then I heard a still, small voice in my head.

"My dear little girl, you know I am with you. I may not help you in the physical world, but I can help guide you in the darkness."

"What darkness, Daddy?"

"The darkness that makes you cry. If you were in the light, you would not be in pain right now. If you walked in the light, you would not fear tomorrow. You would know that you're in complete love at all times. The Father loves you more than any mere mortal man could ever love you.

"Marcie girl, you should know that He holds you near and dear to His heart at all times. He made you and loves you more than you will ever know. He will always have your best interest at heart. Even if it looks like things are not working the way you think, you will never know what He is really doing behind the curtains. Sometimes what really looks bad is really best for you."

"Cho co, mais, Cher what ya be doing out in dis heat?" I jumped from my deep state of mind.

"Oh, T Boy, it's you," I said with an awkward laugh.

"Sorry, Cher, I didn't mean to scare ya."

"It's okay, I was in deep thought," I mumbled with a crooked smile.

"I come to tell ya da news."

"What is it, T Boy?"

"Bill be back."

"What? Where is he?" I was suddenly filled with excitement.

"All I hear is dat he be back," T Boy said.

*How is it that this man who lives deep in the swamps where the light doesn't even shine knows Bill is back, and I didn't know?* "Oh, so he comes back now. Where the hell was he? What was he doing? Why didn't he call? He has totally lost his mind. Well, if he thinks I'm going to run to him, he's got another thing coming." I found myself pacing in front of the willow tree, just ranting and raving. I looked at T Boy and his face said it all. He looked like he was watching a crazy woman. That was when I realized I'd let negative get a hold of me. "I'm sorry, T Boy, I lost control. I'm really, really sorry."

"It be okay, Cher, but you might have to explain to him." He pointed behind me. I turned to see Jim standing several feet behind me.

"Oh, Jim, I didn't see you." I was so embarrassed.

"It's okay, girly." Jim smiled.

"So, ah, how long have you been standing there?" I asked hoping in my heart of hearts not long.

"Long enough to see your ego take control of the situation."

I lowered my head. "I'm sorry."

"I know, Marcie. I'm not here to judge you. That, my girl, is just another lesson that I had to learn. Not to judge people or circumstances by what you see. Only God knows all things. Who am I to judge anyone for any reason?"

"Jim, I think we covered that lesson," I said.

"Are you sure?" Jim asked with one eyebrow arched.

"Mais, I didn't know you had so much smart in ya, Swamp Man." T Boy said.

"It took many years to learn." Jim smiled. "I guess that's why they call me a wise old man."

"Naw, they call you crazy." T Boy grinned, and we all started laughing.

I could feel another lesson coming on. *Yep, here it comes.*

"In my case, your whole way of looking at things changes the older you get. Ego stops getting in the way more when you get older, but of course not with all people. It's not that we lose the drive for life when we get older. We have found that true joy is from within and not in all the material things of the world. When you're young, you work and work to have the car, the house, the boat, and the whole nine yards. Even if you have attained all that, you still will not be happy inside. Then when you start getting older, you start getting rid of all the things you bought that you thought would make you happy. You start downsizing. Your kids are grown and gone, and you have this big empty house. So what you wanted before now has changed. Some people even sell their house and start renting again, and there are even some people who just keep the big house even though they don't need it, still holding on to the past. So who is right? Is it the one who sells it all or the one who stays in the big house? Neither is right nor wrong. Just saying, who can judge any circumstance? Life changes with every breath.

"Marcie, just don't judge Bill."

"Judge him? How can I judge him when he hasn't been here?" I said, flustered.

"You forget I just heard you. You've already decided you're not going to run to him, and he has lost his mind."

I giggled. "When you're right, Jim, you're right. I really have judged him and the situation. Man, how do you do it?"

"What?" Jim asked.

"How do you hold it all together all the time?"

"Well, one thing is I don't hold it together all the time. Second, what you see in me has not always been. I had a long road to get to this. And by no means am I perfect. I just try being conscious of my thoughts and feelings."

"We are all alike; we just don't realize how much. The only difference is we are all brought up different. We are taught different things that can hinder our growth in life. Which by the way, is really not wrong, but just makes getting to our full potential a little harder and a little longer. Our soul will be ready for truth when the time is right. When God is ready for you to know something, He will put the right people in your life. You will have what they call coincidences. Like when God is trying to get your attention, you will hear the radio say something and then later the same day hear someone else say the exact same thing. Just pay attention to everything in your life, stay in the moment, and you will know what the Spirit wants you to know."

"Well, Jim, I just don't know what to do about Bill. The only thing I know is I can't see him and let him hurt me. Would you go talk to him? Just find out where he stands so I know where I stand."

"Yes, little girl, I will go and talk to Bill for you and see what's going on in his mind."

"Oh, thank you so much." I was so excited I just had to hug his neck.

"Now, Marcie, can we please get out of this heat?"

"Yes, yes, of course."

As we walked back to the house, Jim said, "Just give me a couple of days, okay?"

"Sure, take your time, but"—I paused and looked at him—"hurry up."

Jim smiled back at me and gave me a wink. "You got it. By the way, where did T Boy go?"

"Well, sometimes, Jim, you do get a little long-winded, and T Boy is not too much into conversations. So he left when you started your lesson."

Jim cocked his head and me and smiled. "I know I do get carried away sometimes, don't I? I'm sorry."

All I could do was smile.

# CHAPTER 14

I was working at the restaurant when Jim walked in. He pulled up a chair at the table closest to the door, sat down, and winked at me. I headed toward him with a menu.

"To what do I owe this visit, Jim? I've never seen you here." I was happy to see him.

"You know I'm not much on crowds of people," he mumbled, wringing his hands.

I had never seen Jim nervous like this. "So I gather you're not here to eat."

"No, Marcie, not this time. When do you get off?" he asked.

"In about an hour."

"Okay, I'll meet you outside in an hour."

"Is everything all right?"

"Sure, sure. I'll see you then." He immediately got up and went out the door.

I had no idea Jim was so uneasy in crowds. He went to my birthday party. But of course he was sitting in the corner by himself until I sat with him.

Work seemed to drag on forever, but quitting time finally came. I signed out and hung up my apron, said my good-byes, and headed out the door. I held my hand up to block the sun from my eyes and looked for Jim. He was nowhere to be found. I walked over to my old truck and got in. I figured I'd wait for a while.

After what seemed close to forty minutes I started the truck to leave. Just then my passenger door opened, and Bill sat down on the seat next to me.

I was totally in shock to see Bill and not Jim. All I could think was, *Is my hair okay? Is my makeup still on?* Why I was worried about that I'll never know. *I never wore makeup until I got this job. You know, why would this tomboy who fishes, frogs, hunts, and farms want to wear makeup anyway?* Words just would not come up. I couldn't speak. I just looked at him with total astonishment. After months he was sitting right in front of me in my truck.

Bill cleared his throat. "I know you probably don't want to see me, but I hope you'll let me explain myself." After a pause, he continued. "Jim came by to see me today. You know he is really a smart man. He can explain anything so that it seems like the most natural thing in the world. I don't see how a man with that much wisdom would live in the swamps of Louisiana as a recluse. You know what I mean?"

I really didn't know if he wanted a response from me or not, so I continued to look at him wordlessly.

"Marcie, hon, I … I don't know where to start." He paused again. He dragged his fingers through his hair and rubbed his face.

"Okay, here goes. When I was about 13 years old, a couple of boys and I went to sleep in the woods down the road in Moncla, at the oxbow on Red River. It was said that it was Indian land and haunted. Well, I didn't believe in that at all. But nonetheless we packed our tents and gear and got on our bikes and left for the night. It was a long bike ride. None of our parents worried about us going out at night. We never told them where we were really going. I guess they just thought we were camping in the backyard at our friend's house."

"The land had been used has a dump for the city for years. We walked past the dump part and went to the oxbow. We set up camp and gathered wood for the night and then got to roasting hot dogs. By the time the hot dogs were cooked, it was dark. We just sat around talking about school, girls, and the ghost that was supposed to be on the land. We goofed off, wrestling and chasing each other around the tent. We didn't know what time it was when we climbed in the tent to go to bed.

"Some sounds woke me up in the middle of the night. It seemed like someone walking in the woods close to the tent. You know I'm a light sleeper, and I felt around to see if the guys were still in the tent, and that woke them up. I whispered for them to be quiet and listen. We sat up and held our breath. There it was again, a noise of someone walking. Well, we were men and we were not afraid, so we were going to check this out. All three of us got up and went outside the tent to look around. I didn't see anything unusual, so I put more wood on the fire since it was going out.

"Again we heard movement. We all stood still in the dark trying to adjust our eyes with only a little light from the fire. We seemed to be drawn to the right of the tent. It wasn't very clear, but it looked like people were standing on a small hill there, looking at us.

"They looked like what you might see in the old West. The ladies had skirts down to the ground and tucked in shirts, and some had bonnets on their head. They looked like poor men and woman you would see in a wagon train, you know?

"It seemed in a matter of seconds we saw some Indian braves hiding in the bushes watching the people. It was like they were oblivious to us. Our feet were glued to the ground, and our eyes were steadfast on the scene before us.

"All of a sudden one of the Indian braves looked our way. 'Shit, he sees us,' I said. Just then the Indian brave came running toward us from the woods whooping and hollering, with what looked like a hatchet in his hand. We scattered like dirt. We were screaming and tripping all over ourselves trying to get the hell out of Dodge. Finally, after getting our bearings, we were running out the woods. We left everything behind. I could see the brave gaining speed on us. I could have sworn he was pulling on my shirt. As much as I hate to admit it, I screamed like a girl, which just made all of us run even faster screaming for our lives.

"We had to make it through the woods, through the dump, and out to the road where we left our bikes. We scrambled in the dark, got on our bikes, and raced back home. All I could think of was getting home where it was safe and burrowing into my soft bed. None of us seemed to care who was left behind. We just headed home. I think I was ahead of the pack. I could hear the other boys screaming and hollering about never going back there again, not even to get the tent. As far as I know, Marcie, that tent is still standing there today.

"When I got home, I threw my bike down outside and ran into the house, it was pitch black, and everyone was still asleep. I ran to my room, closed the door, got under the covers, and cried like a baby. The next day when I awoke, my clothes were torn, I had scratches all over my face and arms, and my feet were bloody. I hadn't even realized I had no shoes on. I had nightmares for months after this. In fact, I swear the Indian followed me home, because the nightmares I had after that night seemed so real.

"So needless to say when I saw your dad I freaked out. A part of me knew he was there to help me, but another part of me was so scared I felt myself reliving the fright night at the oxbow. He did show me the way to the hole in the tree. He did help get me out the rain. But Marcie, I'm a man, and to admit fear is really hard. I—" Bill paused, and I could see tears starting to well up in his eyes. "Marcie, I cried. I cried like a baby. I was so scared that night. All I could think of was that damn Indian brave coming after me again. I didn't want you to know how weak a man I was and still am. I couldn't face you."

Bill started to cry right before me. "I'm sorry, Marcie; this is hard for me. It's one of those things that I don't know if I will ever get over. I couldn't see you after the incident with your dad, because I started having nightmares again. I could feel that Indian brave grabbing my shirt. I'll never know who those people were that night or who those Indians were. All I can guess is that the braves attacked the woman and children and killed them. I never went back.

"Sweetheart, I love you more than anyone, and my dream has been to have you by my side for life, but the thought of you talking to your dad just irks me no end. I can't be around that. Do you understand? I can't be with you if your dad keeps coming around. I just can't deal with that. Please understand that I love you and would never hurt you intentionally. If Jim had not come to talk to me today, I don't know that I would have ever come to see you again. But he let me know how much I would be losing if I gave you up."

Tears were coming down my cheeks. I hurriedly wiped them away and acted like I wasn't crying.

Bill reached over and grabbed my hand. "Marcie, please forgive me. The worst part of all this was when I walked away from you, and you asked if I was still your friend, and I didn't answer." Now we were both crying. "I know I hurt you, because my heart was hurting too. To walk away from you that day because of fear, I know is inexcusable.

"It sounds ridiculous for me to have walked away over something that most people don't even believe. I was one of them. But Marcie, I … I'm still afraid."

Finally, I opened my mouth to speak. "Do you think I wasn't afraid the day I first saw my dad on the road? I ran away. I ran away from my own dad. Part of me knew it was him, and something in my mind said, *This is not real—run.* And run I did. It was like running into Bigfoot on the bayou. If I hadn't met Jim living in the woods, I would still be running.

"By the way, Bill, what did Jim say to you?"

"Well, he told me his story about his sister dying and leaving his wife and child to find truth. He told me how much in this world we don't understand. He even tried to convince me not to be afraid. He told me we could work this out if we really loved each other. I was really impressed with him. He seems to be a world of knowledge."

"I know, Bill. Jim is wonderful. I would never have made it through this time if he hadn't been here to help keep me grounded."

I started my story minute by minute and confided all my fears and joys about this unusual time in my life. I didn't even realize we had been sitting in the truck in the shade of the restaurant for over an hour. We talked, we laughed, and we came to an understanding.

We decided to compromise. Bill said that he would try to have more of an open mind on these unusual occurrences and learn as much as he could from Jim. I promised to keep a low key on all the weird things that might possibly happen again.

Bill kissed my forehead. Then he smiled and looked into my eyes. "We still friends?"

"Always and forever," I responded with a smile.

All this time I thought it was all my fault. I had done what Jim said not to do. I judged the situation in fear. Who could have known the true reason Bill had left the way he did? I felt bad for judging the situation in a negative way and not believing God could and would work it out.

It felt good to have cleared the air between us and to finally have Bill in my life again. We both realized that day the importance of good communication in our relationship. No matter how hard it was, we needed to put all the cards on the table. I slowly learned in time to remember to always talk with love and never to condemn or judge any conversation or situation.

# CHAPTER 15

The ice forming on the grass crunched under my feet on this clear November night. The full moon glistened on the ice like diamonds. The cold was penetrating through and through. Since it rarely snowed in Louisiana, seeing Jack Frost on the ground was as close to snow I would ever see, and it gave me the feeling of a winter wonderland. Who would have imagined summer had passed, and Bill and I were closer than ever?

Bill was true to his word. He kept an open mind, and we both were talking with Jim on a daily basis. I also kept my promise not to bring up any weird things. Of course, there really hadn't been anything going on to talk about. Maybe all the ghostly sightings had come into my life for a reason—or for a season, even though my silent talks with Michael were still empowering to me. I knew that probably Bill was hearing his spirit guide too but without realizing it. That was not for me to mention; it might be another lesson for Bill with Jim.

Bill and I were inseparable after that day in the truck, when we talked through the heat of the day, clearing the air between us. I never knew my life could feel so full. Bill was at my house every day helping me do the daily chores and get ready for winter.

My part-time job in town lasted another month or two before I finally decided to call it quits and concentrate more on my chores, Jim's lessons, and, of course, Bill.

My mom was ecstatic about Bill and me. Jim beamed at our new relationship. Even T Boy and Frank were growing and learning from hanging around us.

T Boy and Mary Ann got together and had been dating since summer. Frank was still going to school and looking forward to finishing soon. We still had our get-togethers at the camp and some occasional fishing trips.

Today of all days my mind just seemed to wander from one event to the other until this day. I had to smile to see the path it took to get us to this point in our life. The good and the bad all mixed into one wonderful chapter of our journey. How could I have considered giving up the journey and running away? For a long time I ran from love, not knowing that it was exactly what I needed in my life—not only to be loved but to love. It seemed like my life had taken a 180-degree turn from just a year ago.

Jim said the only way you could see how your spiritual journey had progressed was to look at how far you'd come since the last year. *Are you believing the same way you did a year or two ago? Have you grown or matured in the ways of God, past the things you can see? Do you have a peace inside that you never had before? Or do you hunger for things of the Spirit?*

All of a sudden a voice came to interrupt my thought: "My ways are higher than your ways. You will never come to a full and true understanding of Me. You can taste and see that I am good and am here for your best interest." The voice I heard was so real in my head that I knew it must be a message from God.

"Be still and know that I am God and that I created you for the good of all humanity. All things work together for good because I love you. You are under My complete guidance and will always be. You will learn and grow in Me and know that I walk with you every step of the way. Know that when I say no, it is for your good. I will never leave you or forsake you. I am with you forever, even until the end of time."

*Wow, what just happened? That didn't sound like my spirit guide, Michael. I can tell by the words and the way they were said that this was someone very different and it felt peaceful and loving.*

*Could it be God? I don't know, but how reassuring to know that God is with me and guiding me all the way just like Jim said.*

What a wonderful surprise for such a wonderful, special day.

I could see the lights coming into view as I made my way up the walk to and around the bushes. As I turned the corner, there was my Bill standing and waiting for me. Bill's family, my mom and Jim, T Boy with Mary Ann, and Frank along with some friends from town were here to experience this wonderful night with us.

It was a quiet, crisp, magical night, and above me the flowing strands of lights flickered as they seemed to hang in the air like stars. On each side of the aisle before the trellis were two huge plain glass vases with an array of white and pink flowers cascading to the ground. Bill had draped a white cloth wrapped with white lights over the trellis archway at the end of the aisle. It was straightforward and elegant. This didn't even look like my own backyard.

To think my whole life I never even believed in love. I never knew that I could trust and give my heart away like this, that I could actually trust my heart to someone. But here I was in a simple floor-length off-white gown. The dress had a soft V neck, with no sleeves and a short jacket made of lace that extended past my wrist. The shiny material looked like satin as it elegantly flowed to the ground. I'd never been a girly girl, but I could tell by the look in Bill's eyes that he was totally floored. In fact, it would have taken an hour to pick up everyone's jaws from the ground.

I swore I would never were pink, but my beautiful bouquet was of white baby's breath with small white and pink roses intertwined with lace and ribbon. It was definitely breathtaking.

As I slowly walked toward my Bill, I suddenly felt a cool pressure on my arm. I looked to my right, and there was my dad. He was walking me down the aisle. No one else seemed to see him except maybe Jim, who winked at me with a smile from ear to ear. I couldn't believe it—my dad was really here. Out of the corner of my mouth I whispered, "Dad, I'm so happy you made it. I love you."

"Marcie girl, I'll always be there with you. I'm proud of you, my little girl."

"Oh Daddy, thank you," I whispered.

When I reached the end of the aisle, Bill stretched out his hand to help guide me towards the archway, where the Pastor was standing. Bill looked at me with such love and he whispered, "You look awesome tonight."

I winked at him and raised my dress a couple of inches and looked down to the hem of my dress and showed Bill that I had a pair of Dollar Store pink rubber boots on.

Bill laughed. We both knew the significance of this gesture. The tomboy who would never get married, wear pink, or ever wear a dress was gone. In her place was a woman ready to love and be loved, a woman who would give her life for her childhood friend and do and say whatever it took, in love, to keep her man.

I felt like I was in some dream, watching from someplace else. I was so mesmerized by this event and the love I had for Bill that I didn't hear a word from the pastor. My mind went back to growing up with Bill and the guys. The first time my dad showed us how to shoot a gun, fish, or run lines. Our schooldays and all the bumpy school bus rides together. The day Bill kissed me behind the barn at ten years old, and all our talks under my favorite tree. Before I knew what was going on, the pastor said, "I now pronounce you husband and wife. You may kiss the bride." *Wow, did I say I do? Did Bill? We're married?*

Bill slowly and gently bent down to kiss my lips. He then grabbed me up off the ground and swung me around, bouquet and all, laughing. Everyone stood up clapping. I could hear some hollering and laughing. What a great day. We both turned and ran down the aisle like two crazy kids.

Everyone met up at our favorite spot, right on Spring Bayou. Sure it was cold, but Mom and a lot of townspeople had pitched in to put up a huge tent that was rented from a wedding planner in town. There were tables set up, a DJ, and a generator for lights and a little heat. Once everyone started drinking and dancing, no one complained of the cold.

Bill and I had a beautiful three-layer cake made by a woman in town who had the best cakes in the south. Everything was simple and elegant. It all seemed like a dream.

After about an hour of dancing, eating, and drinking, Jim came up and asked me to dance. As we danced, he smiled at me.

"Your dad is so proud of you," he said with a sparkle in his eye."

"You saw him, didn't you?" I asked.

"I sure did. It's funny, but he even looked dressed for the occasion." We both laughed. "I know that made your day, didn't it?"

"He was there to give me away just like he promised. He told me I would be married to Bill one day, and he was right.

"Jim, I have to tell you about the message I got tonight."

"When did you have time for a message?" Jim smiled.

"Well, it was when I was walking from the house to the wedding." I told my story to Jim and I could tell by the look on his face that this was an unusual occurrence.

"I have heard about such events, but they are unusual. I don't think I have ever heard a message in that manner before. But it sounds like God was reassuring you that you are on the right track."

"It didn't sound like Michael this time."

"Well, it could have been another angel relaying a message from God or possibly an apostle or even an ascended master."

"What's an ascended master?"

"I'm not sure, but I've read that they are highly evolved beings not in physical form."

"But it most definitely sounds like the God Spirit inside each of us. Like I said, I'm really not sure.

"This is really not the time or place for another lesson, but know that there is a lot going on in the spirit world that we may never come to understand until we cross over one day. I believe that humanity has never been alone since day one. We have had guidance by spirit beings of a higher nature from the start. I believe the Great Master, Jesus, has reincarnated every so often to guide us from the beginning. He may not have been called Jesus but I believe He was here with us nonetheless since time began.

"I also believe that life, our spiritual journey here, is like an onion. There are many layers. What I have taught you and Bill is just one layer of many. We are not all on the same level. That's why it is so important not to judge circumstances or other people.

I could have felt very jealous that you got to hear what I believe may have been God Himself when you have just started with this. I know your journey and mine are similar and yet not the same. So I will not let my emotion control what you just told me. But what I will tell you, young lady, is this is your wedding party and a time to have fun, not stand around getting another lesson from this old man." He smiled, "So have a good time tonight. This is your night."

It turned out to be a fantastic night. I could tell everyone was having a great time. Everyone was dancing, even Mom and Jim. The food was great, and more people from town were showing up every minute.

After several hours of partying most of the people had gone home, and it was just the gang left. Bill took my hand and led me outside. He walked me to my favorite willow tree and said, "Just look at that tree. Isn't it beautiful?"

Someone had strung lights around the tree, and it was lit up in twinkling white.

"It sure is, Bill," I said, leaning against him.

"How would you like to have a house right here off the river beside your tree?"

"What, right here?" I gasped.

"I bought the land last week," he said proudly. "This is where we will build our house."

"Oh my God, I can't believe it," I said. "It's my favorite spot in the whole world!"

"I know." Bill smiled down at me. "It's my wedding gift to you, sweetheart." I jumped in Bill's arms and kissed his face from top to bottom.

I could hear laughing behind me. I looked and there was the gang just watching and listening.

T Boy walked up. He said, "Ya know, I always knowed you two would be together."

After I watched him sway for a moment, trying to hold his composure, he said, "The beer be gone, so I'm headed to the house."

We all laughed. We knew that a party wasn't over until the beer was gone. I ran up and hugged T Boy's neck. "Thank you so much for coming. I love you."

"Mais, don't say dat Cher too loud; your old man will hear you." We all laughed again.

I looked around at the others. "We want to thank all of you for making this day special. We love each and every one of you."

Everyone seemed to scatter once they heard the beer was gone. Mom said the cleanup would be later. It was just too late to be doing anything else tonight.

Bill and I walked hand in hand to the house to change clothes. He said he had another surprise for me. He also said we were going someplace special but to be sure and leave on my pink rubber boots.

I couldn't imagine what he had in store for me next, but if he said keep on my pink rubber boots, then we must not be going to town. So I dressed down to my blue jeans and a warm flannel shirt.

Soon Bill was knocking on my bedroom door. "Let's go while we still have a huge full moon out," he said through the door."

I opened the door, and Bill grabbed my hand. "Okay, sweetheart, your chariot awaits." Bill walked me out where Frank was waiting in a horse and buggy.

"What …?"

"No talking, Marcie, just enjoy." Bill helped me into the buggy and then sat beside me. Then to Frank he said, "Laissez les bon temps rouler."

Which meant, "Let the good times roll." It made me wonder what Bill had planned next.

We took a leisurely ride back to Spring Bayou where I could see all kinds of lights at the dock. I smiled. I could see Bill's boat all decorated with lights, streamers, and flowers.

"Who …?"

"No talking, Marcie, you will ruin the surprise." Bill said with excitement in his voice. He jumped off the buggy and helped me down. He then escorted me to the boat and sat me in what looked like a queen's chair. I giggled.

Bill waved at Frank, and Frank returned a wink as he jumped into the boat, and we were off.

The night was so cold in the full moon, and it was so quiet you could hear yourself breathe. The water was still and glassy as we drifted toward Bill's camp. It was magical the way the lights from the boat shone around us, twinkling off the water.

When we hit land, Bill again escorted me off the boat and up to the path where someone had lit some Tiki torches all along the way. When I looked down, I realized the ground was covered in rose petals of all colors.

When the camp came into view, it was shining brightly. The old place had been transformed into a beautifully painted structure with strands of lights up and around the steps. I could only wonder how this could be. *There's no electricity out here.*

Bill quickly grabbed me up in his arms, ran up the stairs of the camp, and burst in through the door.

Then he slowly lowered me to the floor and gently kissed me in a way he never had before. I could feel my body yearning for more. His hands were caressing my back and slowly sliding to my waist where he pulled me close. I was so aroused that my breath caught in my throat. As he gazed deeply into my eyes, I could feel his hands slowly lower even more, squeezing and pulling me even closer until my desires soared. I could hear Bill's breathing deepen with anticipation, and I could feel that he was as excited as I was.

Again he lifted me with his strong arms and back, as if I weighed nothing. With his kiss pressing hard against my mouth, he carried me to the bedroom and softly lowered me to the plush featherbed comforter.

Bill had really outdone himself. He had decorated his camp as a woman would. I wondered if it wasn't the doings of a certain female, like my mom. It just didn't seem that Bill would think to light candles, put flowers everywhere, and have everything look like a picture from a magazine.

He lay down against me and whispered that I was his dream come true. He continued to tell me he had never seen anything as beautiful as I was coming down that aisle. He tenderly kissed me and held me close. His warm lips sliding onto my neck and between my breasts gave me feelings of desire I had never experienced.

Tears of joy moistened my face. There was so much emotion welled up inside me that every touch from Bill felt magnified a hundred times. My breath was caught in my throat with every touch and every kiss. I was yearning for him like never before.

Slowly and tenderly our clothes fell from our bodies like leaves from a tree in the fall.

Being together like this was like being in a dreamy haze where I wanted to stay forever. I was lost in his passion, and I didn't care. Before I knew what was going on, I was enjoying every movement from Bill's body against mine. Slowly, deeply, our passion rose. We were like the gears of a clock moving, breathing, becoming one with each other's spirit, mind, and body, each not knowing time or space. On and on our love continued until we felt our bodies explode in unison with euphoria of unbelievable magnitude.

As the euphoria slowly subsided into an overwhelming love for each other, we continued to hold each other, not wanting to let go.

Bill picked his head up from my chest and looked at me strangely.

"What?" I asked.

He started to laugh.

"What is it?" I demanded.

He said with a twinkle in his eye. "That sure was a lot better than that kiss behind the barn when we were kids."

We both laughed.

When his laughter subsided, he looked me in the eyes and said, "I need to tell you something."

"Okay, what?"

"I saw your dad today," he exclaimed.

"You—you saw my dad?" I said with a worried look on my face.

"He was walking you down the aisle. He seemed very happy to be there. For the first time, I wasn't afraid. It seemed like the most natural thing in the world to see your dad where he should be, next to you."

"I didn't think you had seen him. He just seemed to appear next to me. I felt his presence, and I turned to see him. It really made me feel good to see him on our special day."

"Well, Marcie, I think everyone saw him."

"What? What do you mean?"

"At the reception, Frank, T Boy, and Jim were talking about seeing him. Then your mom showed up and said she saw him too."

"I can't believe it. Everyone saw him, and no one ran away or said anything."

"Like I said, Marcie, it was like he was supposed to be there. It seemed the most natural thing in the world to see him with you."

"Bill?"

"Yes, my love?"

"I love you," I said.

"I know," Bill responded.

"No, I mean I really love you," I said with conviction.

Bill smiled and quietly said, "I really love you too."

"Bill?"

"Yes, dear?"

"We still friends?" I asked with a mischievous smile.

Bill smiled again and said, "Friends to the end, always and forever."

# CHAPTER 16

What a wonderful wedding and honeymoon. It turned out better than I could have ever imagined. In fact, with my stubbornness, I had never let myself imagine anything like this in my life.

It was wonderful to wake up with Bill by my side every morning with a long future of love, and contentment. I could tell that Bill was just as happy. In fact, it seemed the whole world had changed. Who could have imagined that my life would turn out like this?

After a several-day honeymoon at the camp, we were back to our lives. We started building our house. If you ever needed patience, it would be when two people get together to build a house. We were tired and at the end of our ropes every night before bed. Getting things to mesh with the house plans, the building material, the carpenter, the plumbers, the electricians, and all the rest just seemed impossible. I wondered and dreamed if we would ever be finished and moved in. I didn't even seem to have the time to sit under my favorite tree. But today, I made an extra effort to make my way past the construction. I sneaked around behind the workers, ducking and diving behind lumber, crawling past roofing material, running from one mighty oak tree to the next until I was out of sight, as if I were in the movie *Mission: Impossible.* I really felt the need for a Jim lesson. *Please, I need some encouragement!* I yelled in my head.

We had been so busy lately, between the house and keeping up the chores at Mom's, that taking time with Jim, T Boy, or Frank seemed like years ago. How I missed the gang and that part of my life. Bill promised that once the house was finished, we would be back to fishing and having dinner guests at our new house.

Having gone past everyone unobserved, I finally found my spot. What a wonderful day to sit under my tree. It was unusually hot today, but being in the shade was wonderful. *What? I think I feel a breeze.* I was leaning back under the tree with my eyes closed and enjoying the sounds of the swamps. When I opened my eyes, I couldn't believe what I saw. Jim was standing there, just looking at me. *Am I dreaming?*

"Jim, I was just wishing you were here," I said as I sat up. "How wonderful, please, please sit next to me."

"Marcie, it's good to see you too. How have you and Bill been?"

It felt great to have Jim sitting next to me. It was like I could draw energy off of him and get rejuvenated. I paused in thought way too long for Jim.

"Marcie, you're talking to old Jim here. How are you and Bill doing?"

"Well, Jim, to be honest, it seems we don't have time for anything but that house, and we don't exactly agree on much of anything anymore," I said sadly.

"You know what you have to do, don't you?" Jim gave me a raised eyebrow and a crooked smile.

"Yeah, have patience with love," I drawled, rolling my eyes.

He laughed. "Yes, but you also need to take time for the two of you. You should also take time for just you too."

"Well, that is easier said than done. In fact, this is the first day I've managed to escape the construction at the house for some tree time."

"It's also imperative to spend time alone with that Great Universal Energy that we call God. That way you will hear His voice, and He will fill your spirit with the light that keeps us all going. You know, Marcie, when you start feeling down with this house, He will direct your path, as I have said since I met you. Just take time. Take time to listen, feel, touch, and sense Him. He is everywhere all the time.

"I believe that is why you love sitting under this tree so much. You feel the peace of the Great *I AM.* You are grounding with nature and taking on the energy of the earth, the air, the trees, and the water in front of you. It picks you up and gives you a positive feeling." Jim smiled.

"When you're right, you're right. I crave this spot. It does lift my spirit." I cocked my head sideways to get the sun out my eyes from the crack in the tree. "So Jim, what's on your mind? You didn't just happen by, did you?"

"No, I wanted to let you know my plans," Jim announced.

"What kind of plans?"

"I am feeling the need to do a Crocodile Dundee."

"What? What in the world are you talking about?" I asked with a giggle.

"I want to do a walkabout," Jim said.

"I still don't know what you're saying."

"Gee, Marcie, do you ever watch TV?"

"Yes, sometimes," I said wondering what was on his mind.

"Did you ever see the movie *Crocodile Dundee*?"

"Sure I did," I said with a smile.

"Well you remember when …"

I interrupted, "Stop, Jim, I know what you're saying. I was just hoping I wasn't hearing what I thought I heard. So when are you planning to leave?"

"It will probably be the end of the week," Jim said with his head down.

"Does Mom know?"

"No, I'm headed that way now."

"Jim?" I paused.

"What's on your mind, Marcie girl?"

"You … you are coming back, aren't you?" I was dreading what he might say.

"Marcie, of course I am. I have too much here. I not only have my little house, but I have family again, people who accept me for me.

"Do you think that maybe your mom would like this?" He was digging in his pocket and pulled out a small box. When he opened it, there was a beautiful ring.

"Jim! You don't mean it. You want to marry my mom?"

"Yes, Marcie, I love her. Do you think she will consider it?"

"Of course she will!" Tears started forming in the corners of my eyes.

"Once I give her the ring and ask her to marry me, then I'll ask her to wait for me. This is what caused trouble before. My first wife didn't want anything to do with me leaving and growing in the spiritual ways of life. But Marcie, I feel your mom and I are on the same page. Plus I love her very much."

"Oh Jim, I'm so happy. I couldn't imagine anyone else with my mom but you. And I believe you're right: Mom will feel honored to have you, and yes, she will wait for you," I said, wiping a tear from my cheek.

Jim got up and started walking toward Mom's house. He turned and waved, calling back, "Wish me luck!"

I smiled. "You don't need luck, Jim, you have love."

*Oh my God, how I wish I was a fly on the wall.* I was deep in thought when I heard Bill.

"Hey, lazy bumpkin, I knew if I couldn't find you, you would be here."

He sat down next to me, took a blue bandana from his pocket, and wiped the sweat from his forehead.

"Bill, you're not going to believe it. I just saw Jim."

"Really? So what's the old man up to?"

"He's gone to Mom's to ask for her hand in marriage, and he's going on a turnaround," I said, so excited that I couldn't get my words right.

"He's asking your mom for her hand?"

"Yes! Can you believe it, Bill?"

"That's great news. I know your mom needs someone. Everyone needs someone. Now, what else did you say? Did you say Jim is going on a turnaround?"

"Yeah, that's what he said."

"Are you sure he said turnaround?"

"You know that movie *Crocodile Dundee*?" I asked.

"Sure." Then he laughed. "Oh, you mean he's going on a walkabout."

"Yeah, that's what I meant." I giggled.

"You mean he's leaving too? Is your mom going too?"

"No, no, he wants Mom to wait for him."

"Oh, how do you think that will go?"

"Bill, I wish I was there. I just can't sit here; I need to know what's going on. Do you think we could go spy on them?"

"Well, let's walk over there. He's had enough time." We got up and walked toward Mom's house hand in hand.

As we walked into the house, I could hear Mom crying. I looked at Bill. "Oh no."

"Calm down, Marcie, it might not be that bad."

"I haven't heard Mom cry like that since Dad died," I said, worried.

We slowly walked around the corner into the living room. There stood Jim holding Mom. Bill cleared his throat. Mom looked up, tears streaming down her face, with the biggest smile I'd ever seen.

"*Mom?* Are you all right? Are you okay? Why are you crying?"

"Marcie, I'm getting married," Mom blurted out. "I'm just so happy."

"Man, you scared me."

"It's okay, Marcie. Once Jim gets back, we will start planning our future. He wants me to wait for him, and you know I will." Mom was beaming with joy.

I looked at Jim. He had a peaceful smile that could not be compared to any look I'd ever seen on his face. I could see in his face the acceptance he had always wanted in his life. We all loved Jim just as he was, never turning our backs just because he was different.

I looked at Bill, who winked at me and said, "Told you so."

"Oh hush, know-it-all." We both laughed. What a great day this turned out to be. Just then I could hear a voice inside say, "Marcie, that's the way it should be. It was never intended for people to have any division from each other or from our Maker. It was the intention of our God from the very beginning of time that we walk in the garden of His presence forever. Let your love pour out; never be afraid, and know you never walk alone."

Jim was looking at me. He leaned over and whispered in my ear and said, "I heard that too."

We both smiled.

"Jim what do you think it meant when He said 'the garden of His presence'?"

"Marcie we're like waves in an ocean, and even though we are never apart from out wonderful Maker, the waves are always crashing on the shore? Think of the wave as the human body. Try to think of a time when you were one with God. You know, when you leave this human body—either when you're in meditation in that private inner room with just you and your Maker; or in deep prayer; or even when you leave this earthen body altogether—that is when that wave no longer has to feel the urge to crash on the shore but instead wants to melt into the whole. When the waves stop altogether and there is complete stillness and peace.

"When you and Bill merged together as one was it not wonderful? Just think of merging with the Father of all creation, not in a physical way but in a spiritual way. You will not have to fight or struggle anymore. You will be at complete peace beyond all understanding. The ocean will be calm. You will have reached your goal, the core of the onion, or you could say the inner depth of the fullness of God.

"It is a struggle every day to put aside the human nature and come to a complete understanding of who you really are and putting aside the flesh to love beyond. Jesus, one of the greatest masters ever known accomplished this. That is our goal. It could take many lifetimes to merge with the Father on a permanent basis.

"Marcie, I believe we lost a part of our true nature, or maybe not lost it but forgot our true nature, when we came to this human body in the beginning, and we have been trying to find our way back ever since. We're like small children getting lost in a big department store. They get sidetracked by some toys and start playing, looking around, maybe play with other kids in the store, and they have no idea they are lost. They just play and have a good time. Then suddenly they realize they are alone with just the toys, and Mom and Dad are not there. Children can go a long time without even realizing they are lost. But eventually they do finally realize something is missing, and they go searching for it. Imagine the joy they find when they see their parents, the reunion they have with each other. Ah, what a glorious time that is.

"That's why I say our purpose is to find that place again in oneness with Him. God loves us so much that He has never left our side, even though we get sidetracked and walk away and go play with some toys. He has never ever left us. He has never stopped loving us. He is waiting patiently on us.

"Marcie, what does the God of the universe do with forever? He waits on His true love—on us—to return to the garden of His presence. That's why I feel, if you heart is on the right track, that there is no wrong. We will always make mistakes, turn left when we should have gone right, but Love waits patiently for us at all the wrong turns.

"Do you remember in the Bible where it says every knee will bow? What I believe that means is, at one time or another we will come to that place of complete acceptance in the God of the entire universe. Remember free will? It was our free will that took our attention off our goal, and it will be free will that brings us back. You will always have this yearning inside that cannot be fulfilled by anything but the oneness of God. But my dear Marcie, we are on our way."

Jim fell silent, and we looked around. Bill and Mom were still there listening and hanging on every word. It seemed we all just stood in remembrance of a time beyond this one, a time in the beginning with God. You could feel rightness in the air, as if the whole universe stood silent to give His blessings on what was being said.

Bill cleared his throat. "Wow, that was beautiful."

Mom nodded and said, "That's why I love this man." She reached out and grabbed Jim's arm. "He always sends out such love and peace."

Bill spoke up again. "I don't mean to change the subject, but you know, I've been listening to y'all for months now, and it feels like I'm really starting to understand more. I'm seeing some connections that have been made."

We all just stood there waiting to understand what Bill was trying to say.

"Remember, Marcie, the night we went frogging?"

"Sure I do."

"Remember how you told me not to forget my knife while we were sitting under your tree, and I told you not to forget your pink Dollar Store rubber boots?"

I giggled softly. "Yes, I definitely remember that."

"You never told me that before. Well, that stuck with me for some reason. Every time I left the house after that, I could hear you say not to forget my knife.

"The night we went to run fishing lines, I left the house without my knife. I was in the truck and was headed down the driveway when I heard your voice, 'Don't forget your knife.' I drove back up the driveway, retrieved my knife in a hurry, and headed to the dock.

"Marcie that night when I dove in the water after that alligator took you under, I left that knife in the boat where I was sitting. All I had was my bare hands. I blamed myself for not remembering that stupid knife.

"Anyway, to make a long story short, for some reason T Boy had dropped his knife on the path to the dock that night. If I hadn't brought that knife and had it sitting on the seat, T Boy wouldn't have had a knife handy to jump in to kill that gator."

Jim smiled. "I remember that. I saw T Boy reach for his knife and it wasn't there, and he then took yours."

"Marcie, I normally keep my knife in its sheath attached to my belt, but I was in such a hurry I left it home and only grabbed the knife. That's the only reason it was sitting on the seat. The way it all worked out is why you're alive today. I can't help but think someone or something had a hand in this."

Jim was totally excited. "This is exactly what I have been saying all this time, and now you see it. There are no accidents that God does not know about. I believe our lives are planned out. That night was a turning point in your and Marcie's relationship. It may have taken something as awful as a gator attack to wake you two up, but see how everything fits together?"

It felt like the light went on in everyone's mind at the same time. We all stood in silence reliving the event. The knife, the gator, the hospital … it was all planned to get me where I was today.

The synchronistic events from the last several months boggled my mind. As I thought on it, it all started with one simple request: "Don't forget the knife." *Bill leaves his house, remembers he left his knife; goes back to get it, but leaves the knife sheath behind so that the knife is on the seat of the boat. T Boy grabs the knife and kills the gator. I end up in the hospital with Bill by my side, and I start seeing Bill in a different way. Wow, this is amazing.*

It felt like we were all blown out of the water. I started to giggle.

"What's so funny, Marcie?" Jim asked.

"I can see this stupid look on everyone's face like we just found a hidden treasure or something."

We all laughed because it was true. We'd unlocked a mystery of the universe that most people didn't even realize.

# CHAPTER 17

Several months later, as I sat under my favorite willow tree by the water's edge with my new house behind me, my mind unfolded like a blanket of time full of all the memories since my dad left. I'd learned so much since that day. My journey and I had become good friends.

I had written down the lessons in a journal from my good friend Jim, the crazy voodoo swamp man of Louisiana. I had to smile at myself to think how ridiculous this was, but I along with a whole town had feared this gentle man of the swamps. How quick we'd been to judge someone before we'd even met him.

This journal will always hold some of the greatest mysteries of life. I know that one day my kids or my grandkids will ask me questions about this time in my life and why I feel the way I do; or they will ask themselves the very same questions we all ask ourselves: Why are we here? What is my purpose? I will sit with my family and go over this journal in hopes that they will understand and come to see what a wonderful life we lead.

Jim had recently returned from his journey with a promise of the revelations he uncovered. He would bring a wisdom beyond our natural minds to share with us.

I asked Jim when I saw him the other day why my dad hadn't been around in a long time. He explained, "Well, Marcie girl, it's possible that he was needed for just a season to help you and your mom, and now he has reincarnated again to this plane, or maybe he is just learning and growing on the other side. His journey is probably not finished yet, and he has a lot to accomplish." I nodded and agreed with him.

"I knew I would find you here, sweetheart," Bill said, walking up to me. I jumped from my deep thought realm.

"Are you almost ready to go? I'm really in the mood for some of those pork dinners at the Cochon de Lait."

Every May, there was an outside pig roasting on the Bayou we called Cochon de Lait, a tradition that went back for generations. Pork dinners included rice dressing, yams, coleslaw, and a roll. Pigs were slowly roasted, split down the middle, and wired open so the fire would cook them inside and out. These prepared pigs were hung from a tree or some Cajun get-up, close to an open fire. In the old days the men would be using an old cane pole to turn the pig slowly for hours on end as it roasted. This method locked in all the juices and gave the outer skin a crisp layer of pure heaven. It was a lot of hard work, but it was also the best pork you'd ever sink your teeth into.

Bill reached a hand to help me up. "Are you writing in your journal again?"

"No, just going over some of the lessons Jim taught us. I really missed him when he was gone and hope he doesn't go anywhere anytime soon."

"Don't worry; he'll probably stay a good while. He and your mom have a wedding to plan, you know," Bill said with a wink.

"I'm really excited to see what other lessons he learned on his journey." I shook my head to get my hair out my face. "You know, he didn't even say where he went on his walkabout."

"He probably didn't know where he was going either, and he's probably waiting for the right time to tell us everything."

For the first time in my life I felt like I was in complete alignment with the universe. I knew why I loved Louisiana, with its unbearable humidity and its Cajun culture. I knew why I loved Bill and Jim, my mom and all my friends. I knew why dad had come back to show me how to love, and I knew and saw how every event brought me closer to God.

As Bill and I walked away from my favorite tree hand in hand, we knew with complete acceptance that everything in life would be all right. *After all, God is in control.*

"Bill?" I asked.

"Yes, my sweetheart," Bill answered.

"We still friends?" I asked with a wink and a smile.

Bill laughed, "Always and forever."

# THE END

# AFTERWORD

As I mentioned in my acknowledgment, this book never would have been written at this time if I hadn't gotten my first channeled message from my angels through Kim O'Neill.

We may live our whole lives never knowing our purpose on this earth, but Kim not only told me that my first book would be dictated to me by my angels, but she told me to have a writing schedule, and told me how long it would take to complete my first book. To my surprise, this all came to pass.

I followed her instructions, and by day two, a story started to unfold. Every night was exciting and kept me on the edge of my seat, wanting to know what would happen next. I laughed and cried each night watching Marcie's life unfold.

I'm not going to say that no part of this book reflects me, since I do live in Louisiana close to the swamps and bayous, and I have fished, hunted, and gone frogging. Still, my angels gave me the characters and this great story line. I've had unusual experiences from the other side most of my life, and even more opened up to me several year before my sister died. There is no doubt in my mind that we are always in the presence of angels.

Louisiana Cajun Girl is just the beginning. There is a world of imagination waiting to unfold in the pages of the many books to come.

If each person who reads this book walks away with just a small amount of inspiration, then this book has succeeded in what it was meant to accomplish.

Printed in the United States
By Bookmasters